Mimi and the Cutie Catastrophe

Shauna J. Grant

graphix

An Imprint of

SCHOLASTIC

This book is dedicated to
my younger self and every child
following the magic inside their heart

Library of Congress Control Number: 2021937770

ISBN 978-1-338-76667-7 (hardcover)
ISBN 978-1-338-76666-0 (paperback)

10 9 8 7 6 5 4 3 2 1   22 23 24 25 26

Printed in China 62
First edition, July 2022

Edited by Megan Peace
Book design by Shivana Sookdeo
Creative Director: Phil Falco
Publisher: David Saylor

CONTENTS

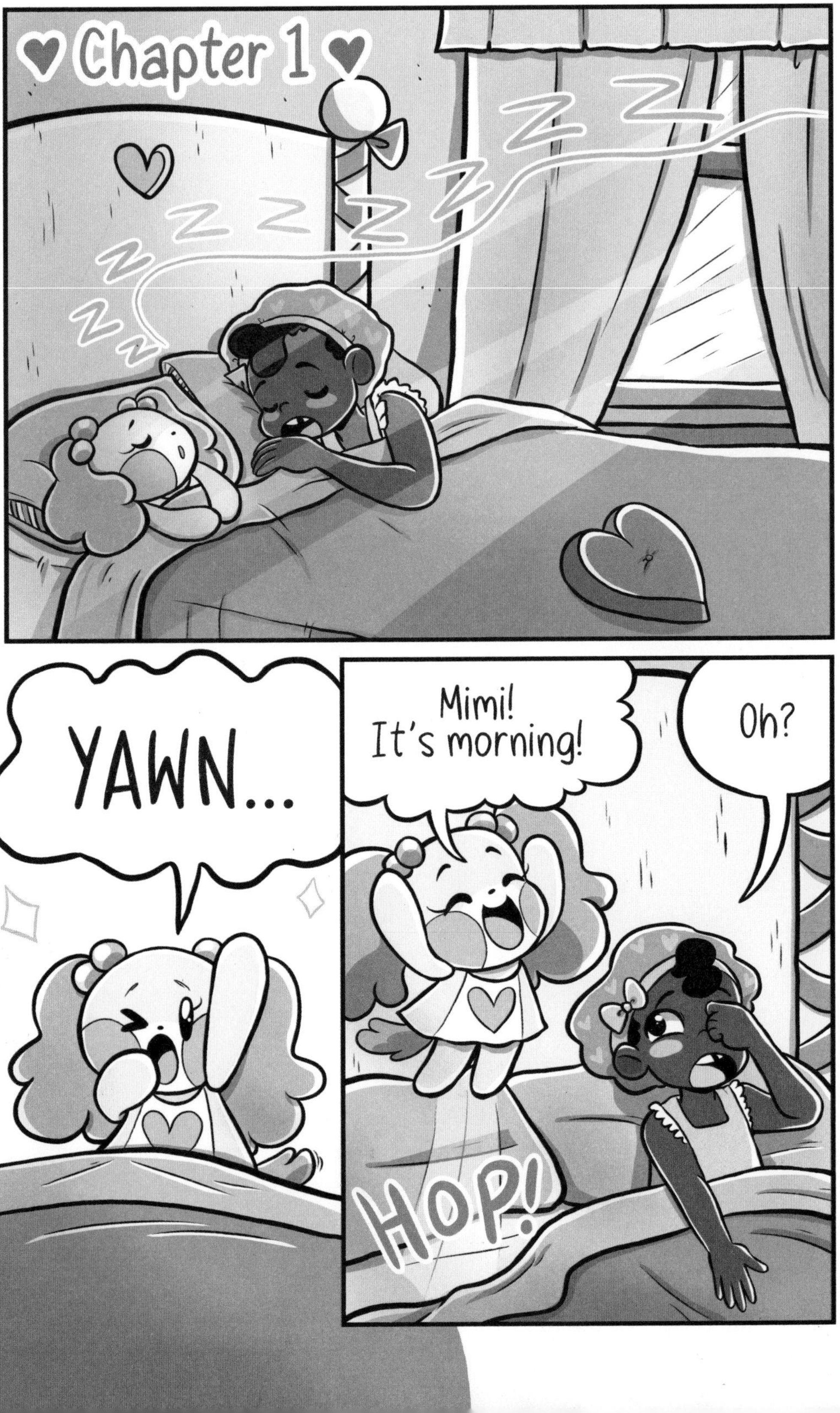

Chapter 1
YAWN...
Mimi! It's morning!
Oh?
HOP!

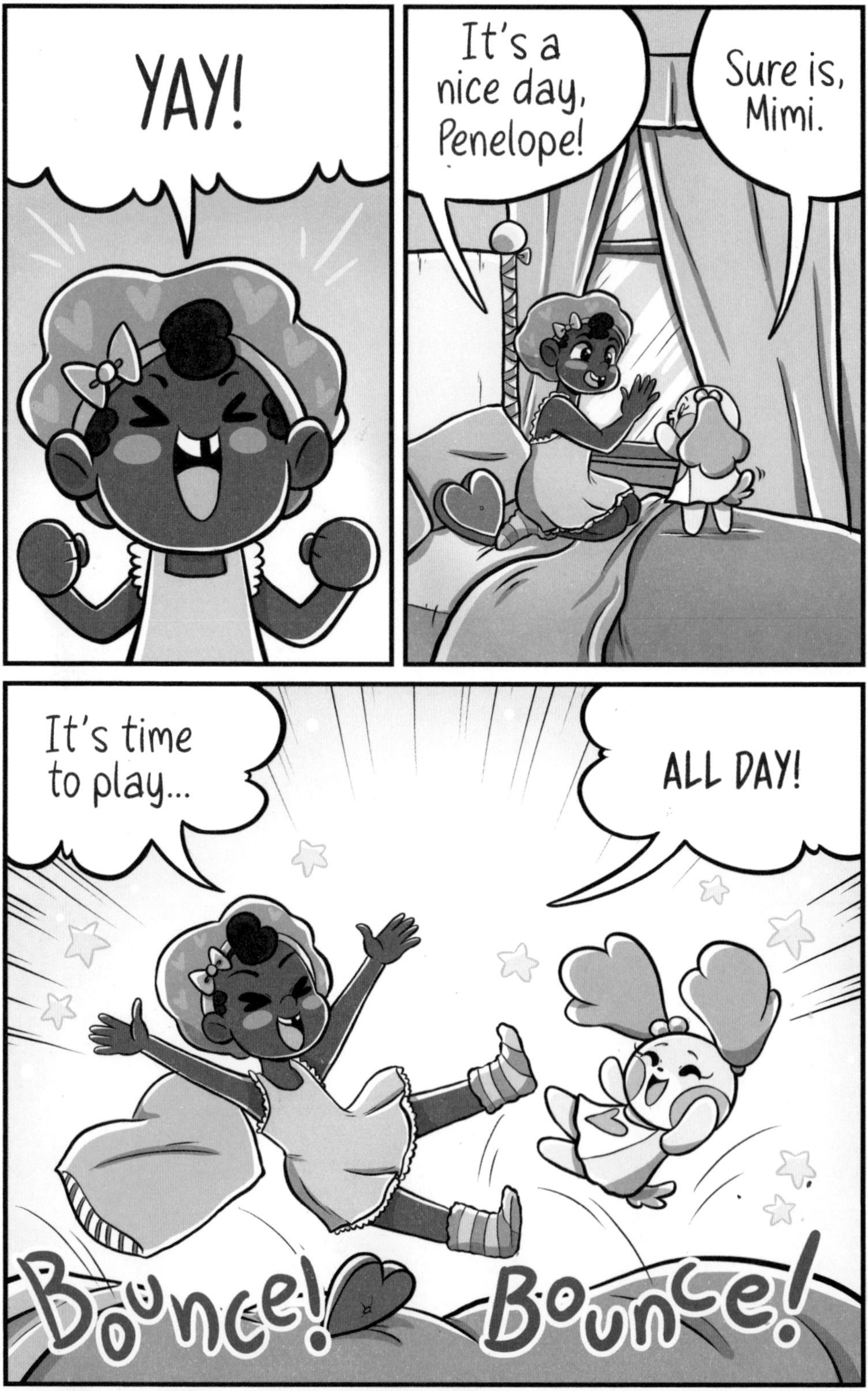
YAY!
It's a nice day, Penelope!
Sure is, Mimi.
It's time to play...
ALL DAY!
Bounce! Bounce!

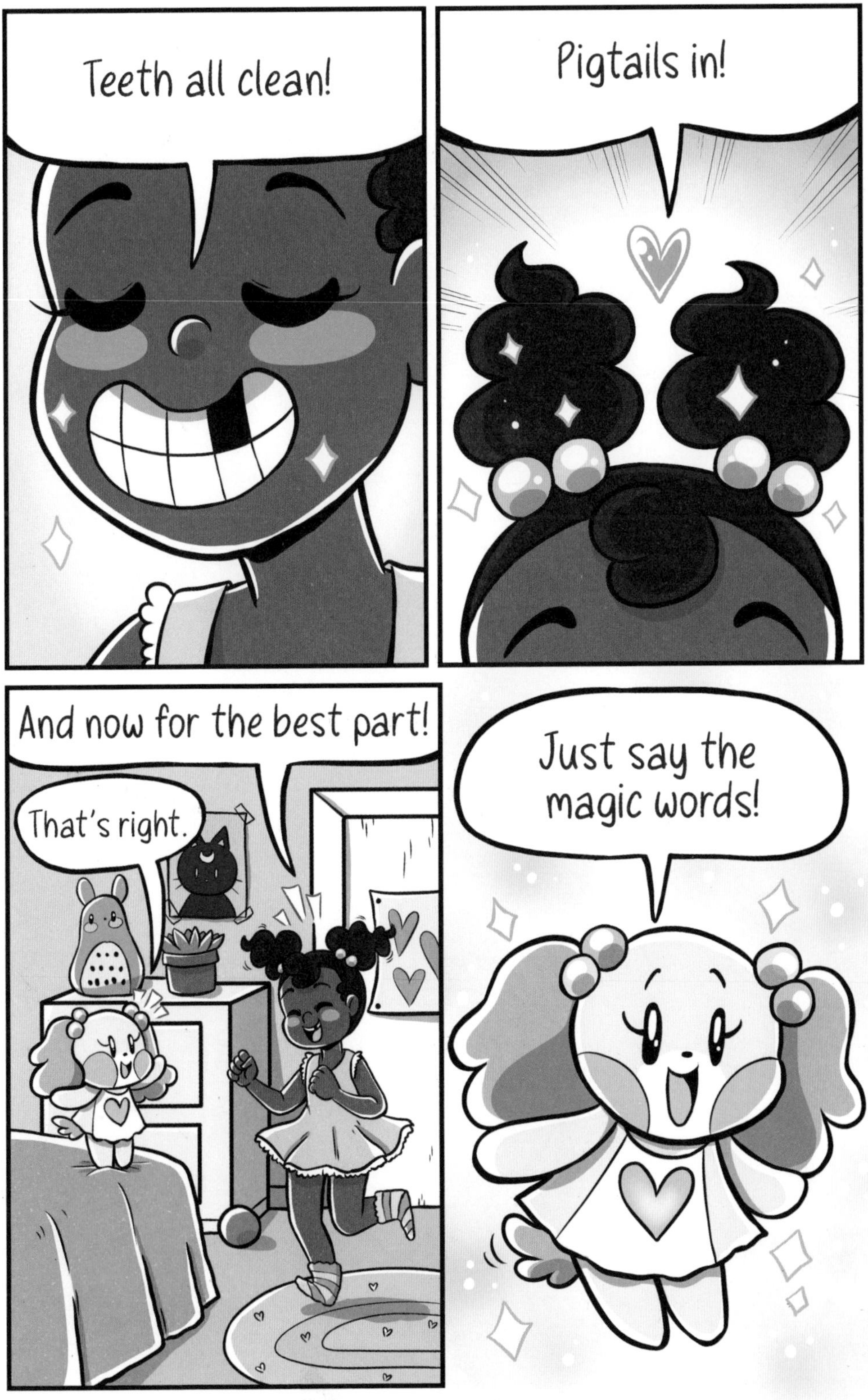
Teeth all clean!
Pigtails in!
And now for the best part!
That's right.
Just say the magic words!

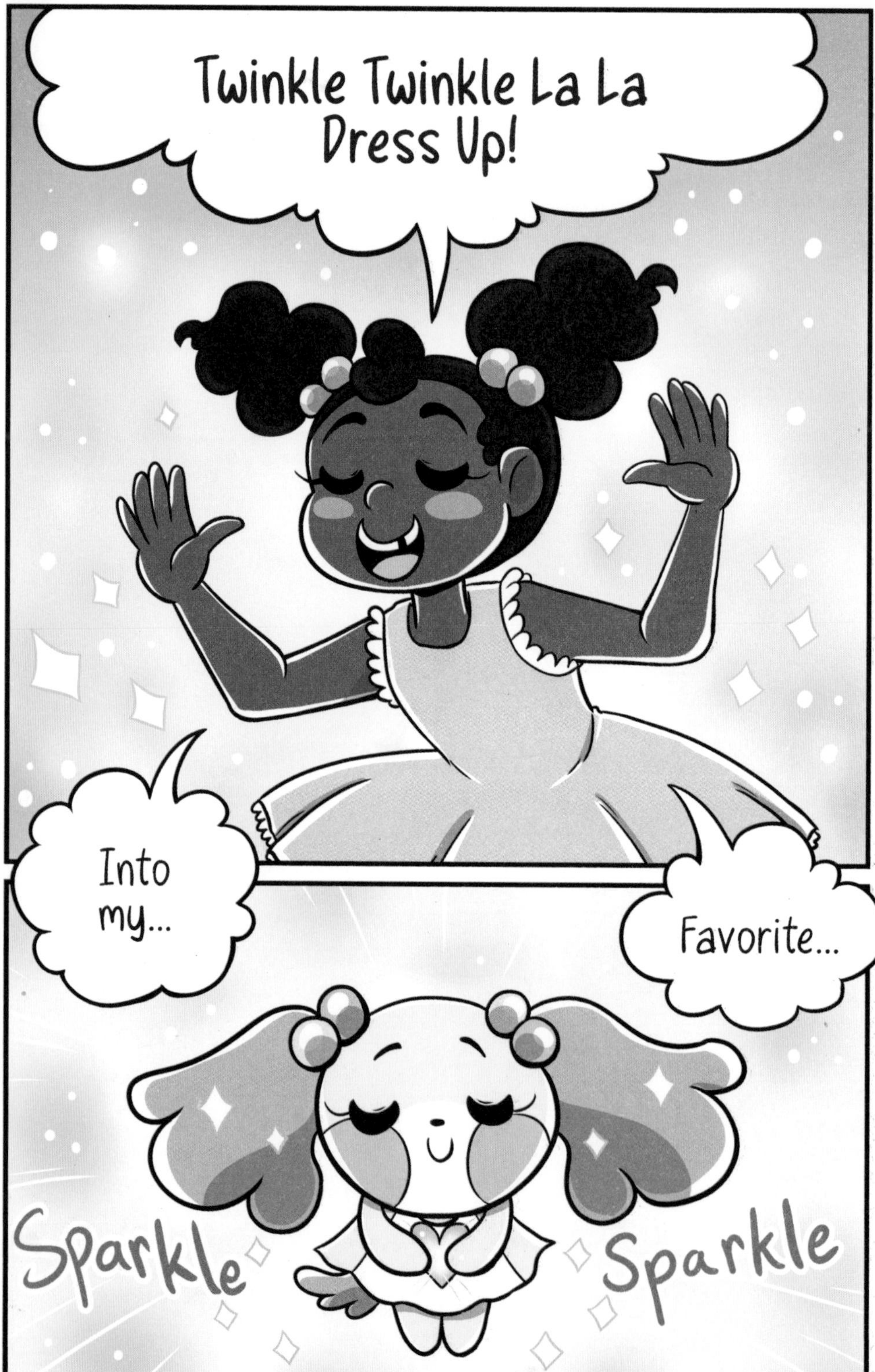
Twinkle Twinkle La La Dress Up!
Into my...
Favorite...
Sparkle Sparkle

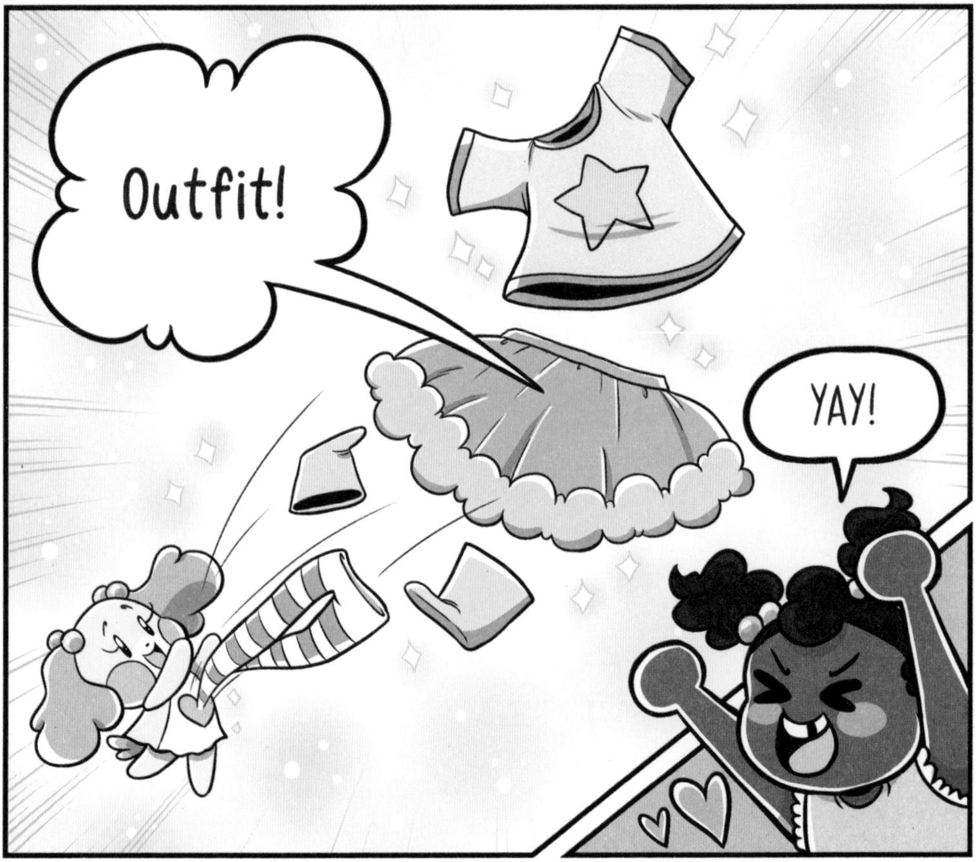
Outfit!
YAY!

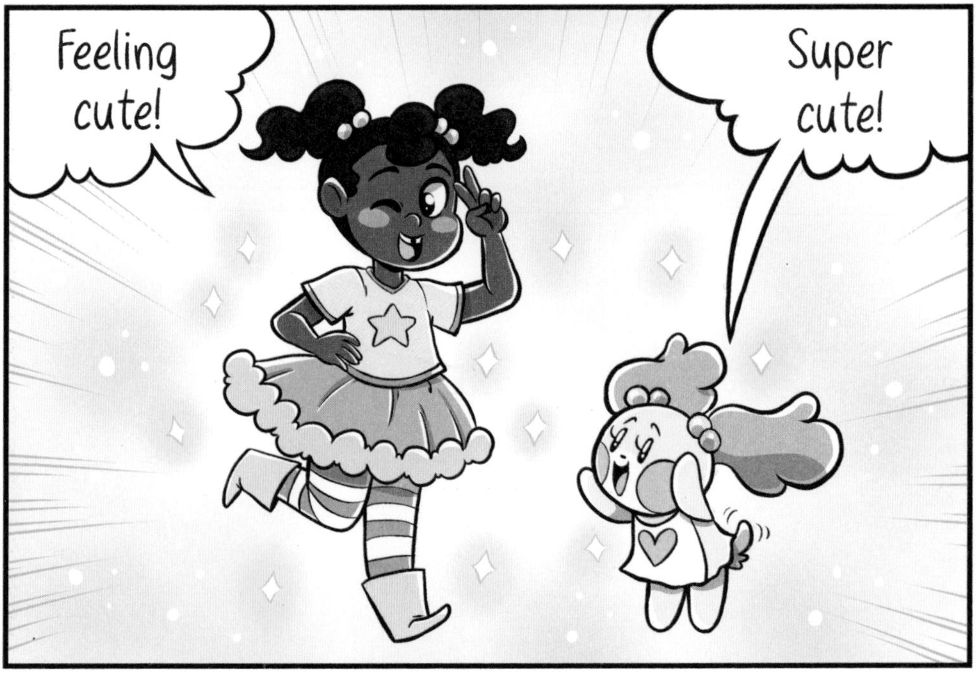
Feeling cute!
Super cute!

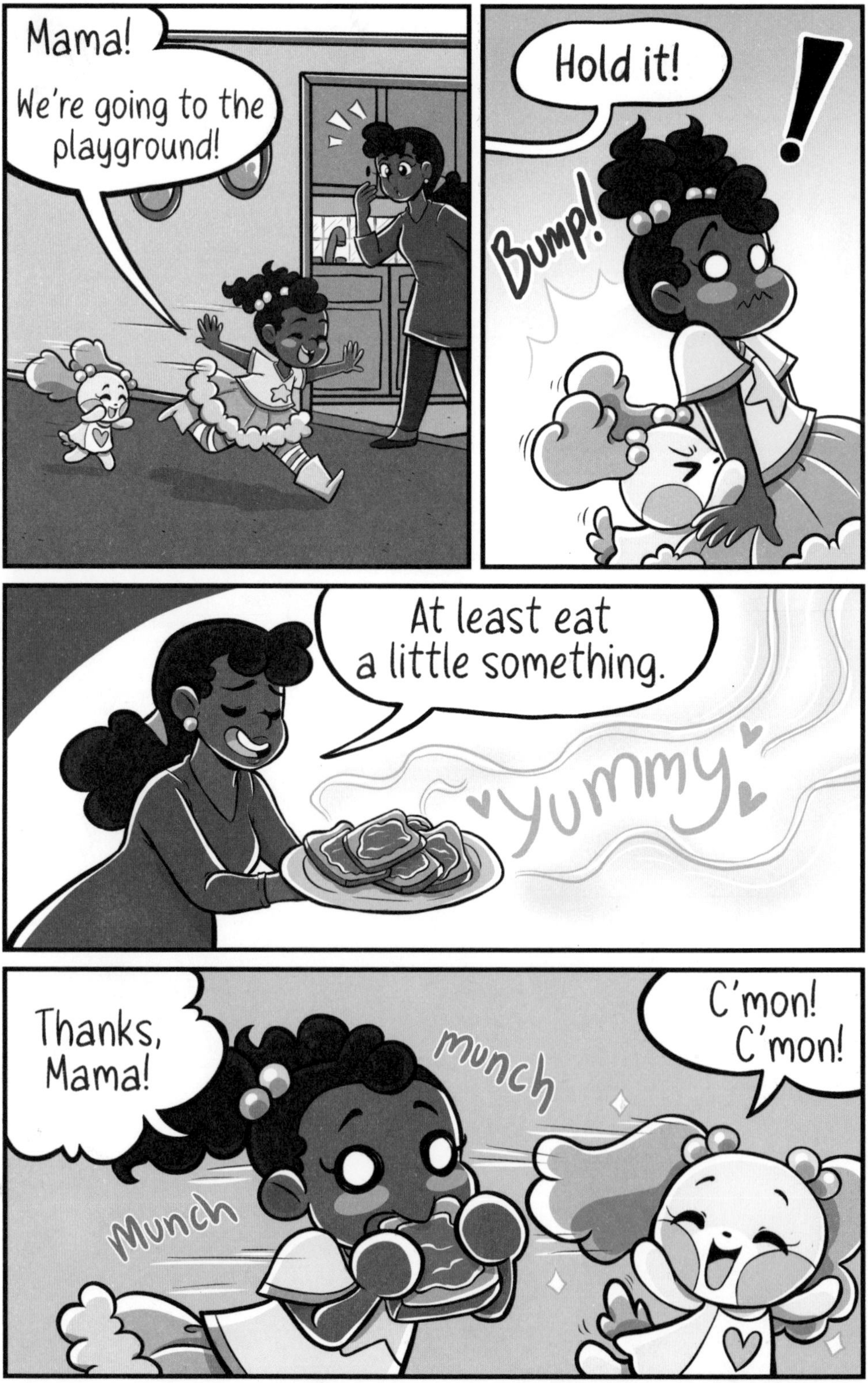
Mama!
We're going to the playground!
Hold it!
!
Bump!
At least eat a little something.
yummy
Thanks, Mama!
munch
Munch
C'mon! C'mon!

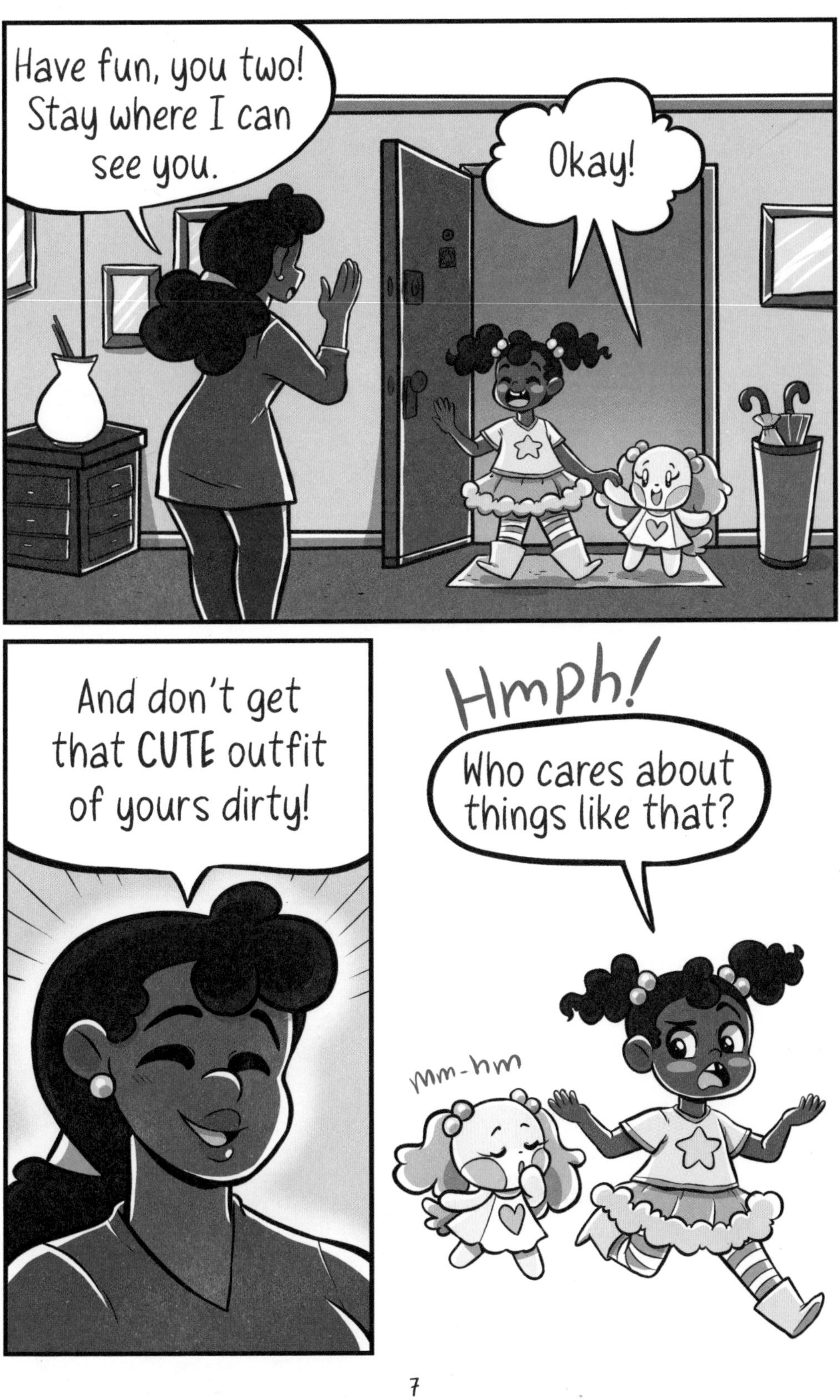
Have fun, you two! Stay where I can see you.
Okay!
And don't get that CUTE outfit of yours dirty!
Hmph!
Who cares about things like that?
mm-hm

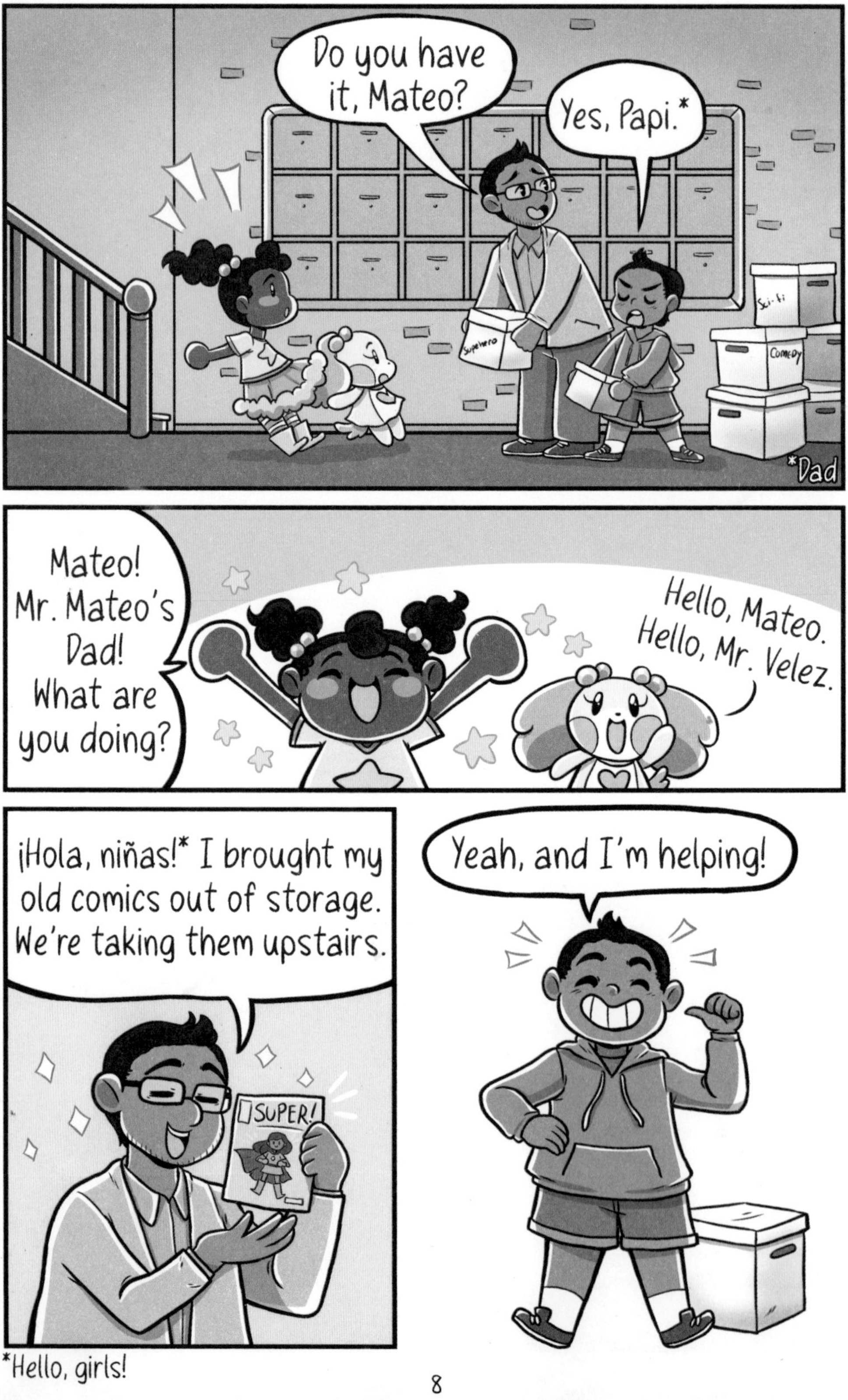
Do you have it, Mateo?
Yes, Papi.*
Superhero
Sci-fi
COMEDY
*Dad
Mateo! Mr. Mateo's Dad! What are you doing?
Hello, Mateo. Hello, Mr. Velez.
¡Hola, niñas!* I brought my old comics out of storage. We're taking them upstairs.
SUPER!
Yeah, and I'm helping!

*Hello, girls!

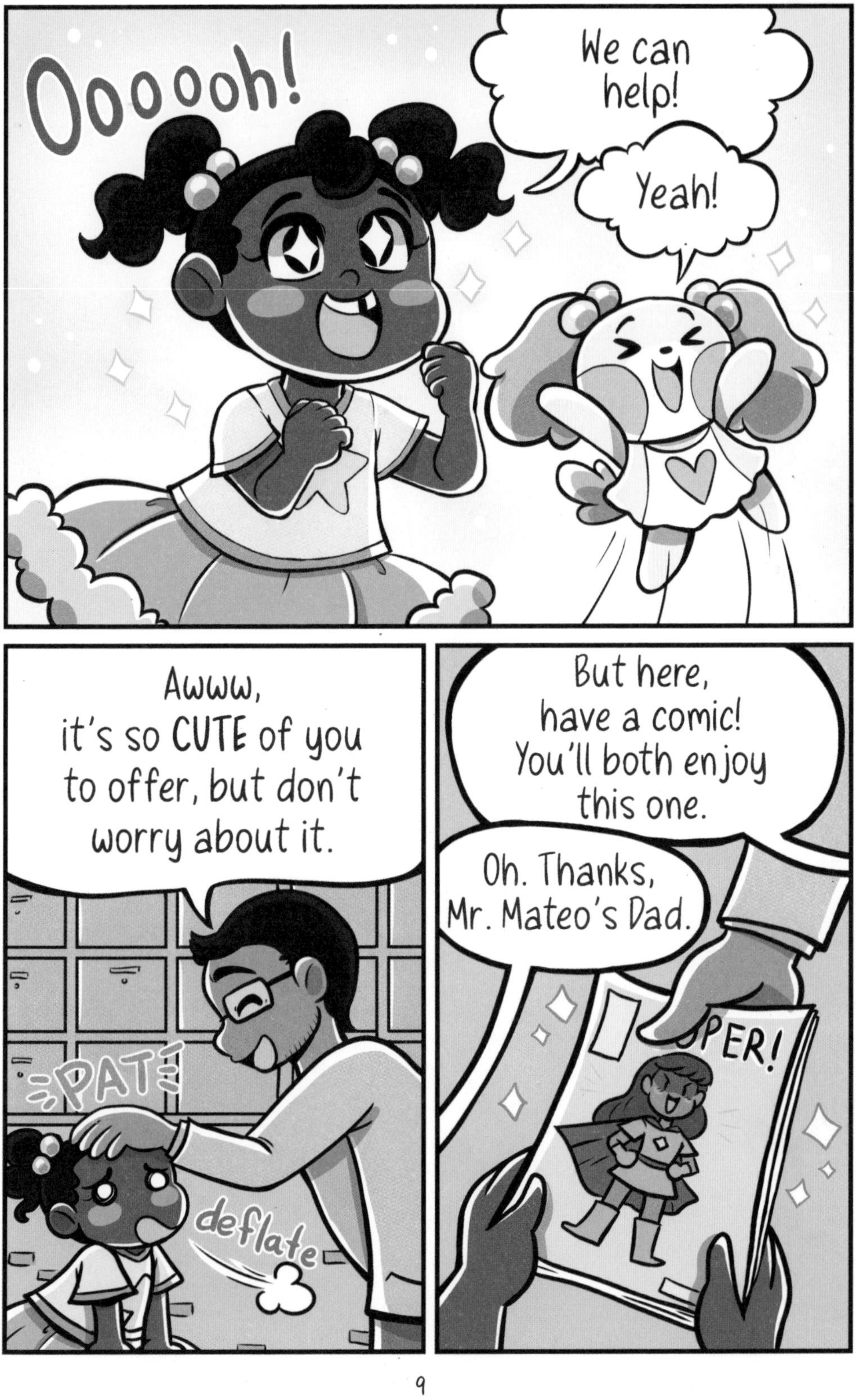
Oooooh!
We can help!
Yeah!
Awww, it's so CUTE of you to offer, but don't worry about it.
PAT
deflate
But here, have a comic! You'll both enjoy this one.
Oh. Thanks, Mr. Mateo's Dad.
PER!

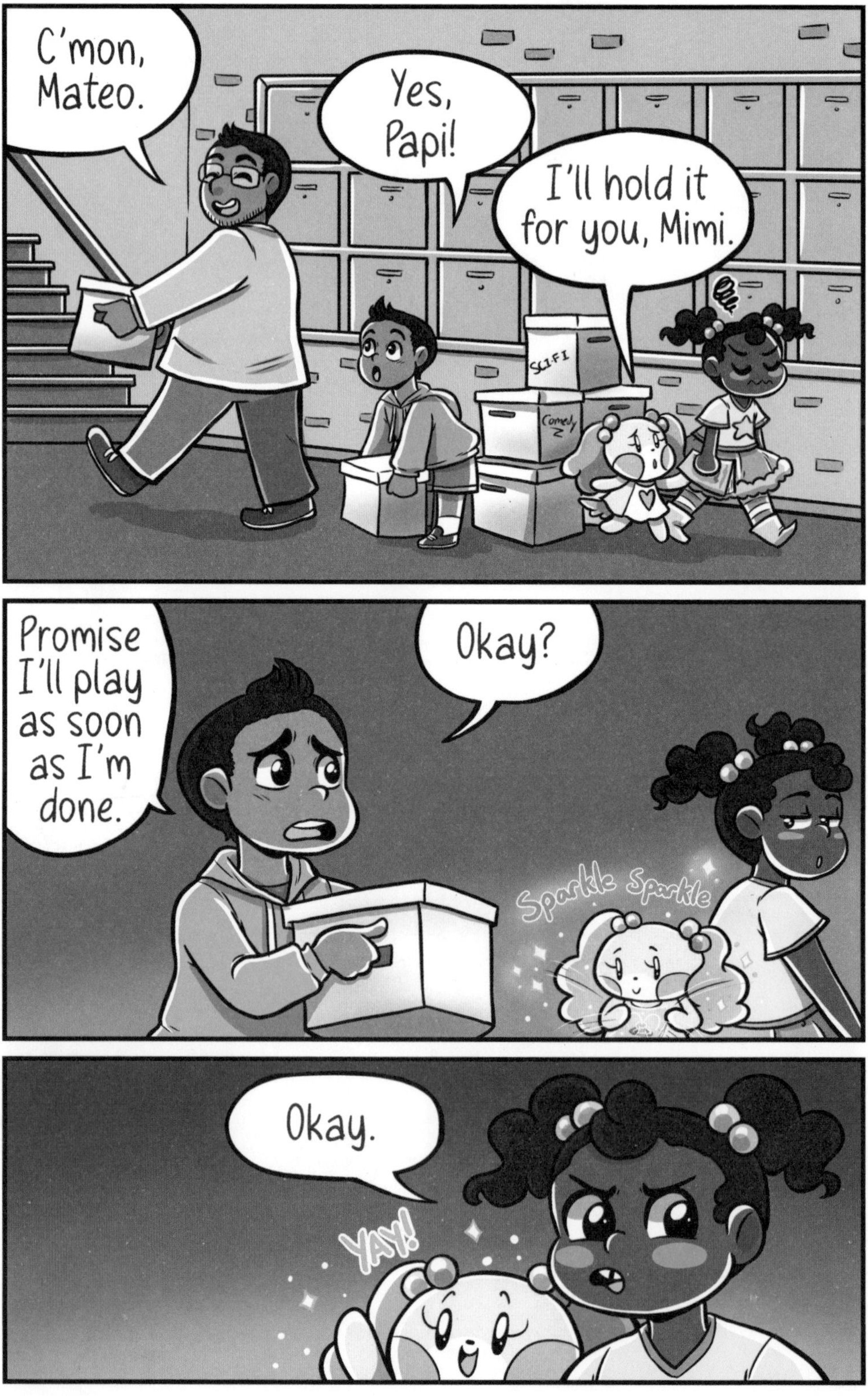
C'mon, Mateo.
Yes, Papi!
I'll hold it for you, Mimi.
SCI-FI
Comedy
Promise I'll play as soon as I'm done.
Okay?
Sparkle Sparkle
Okay.
YAY!

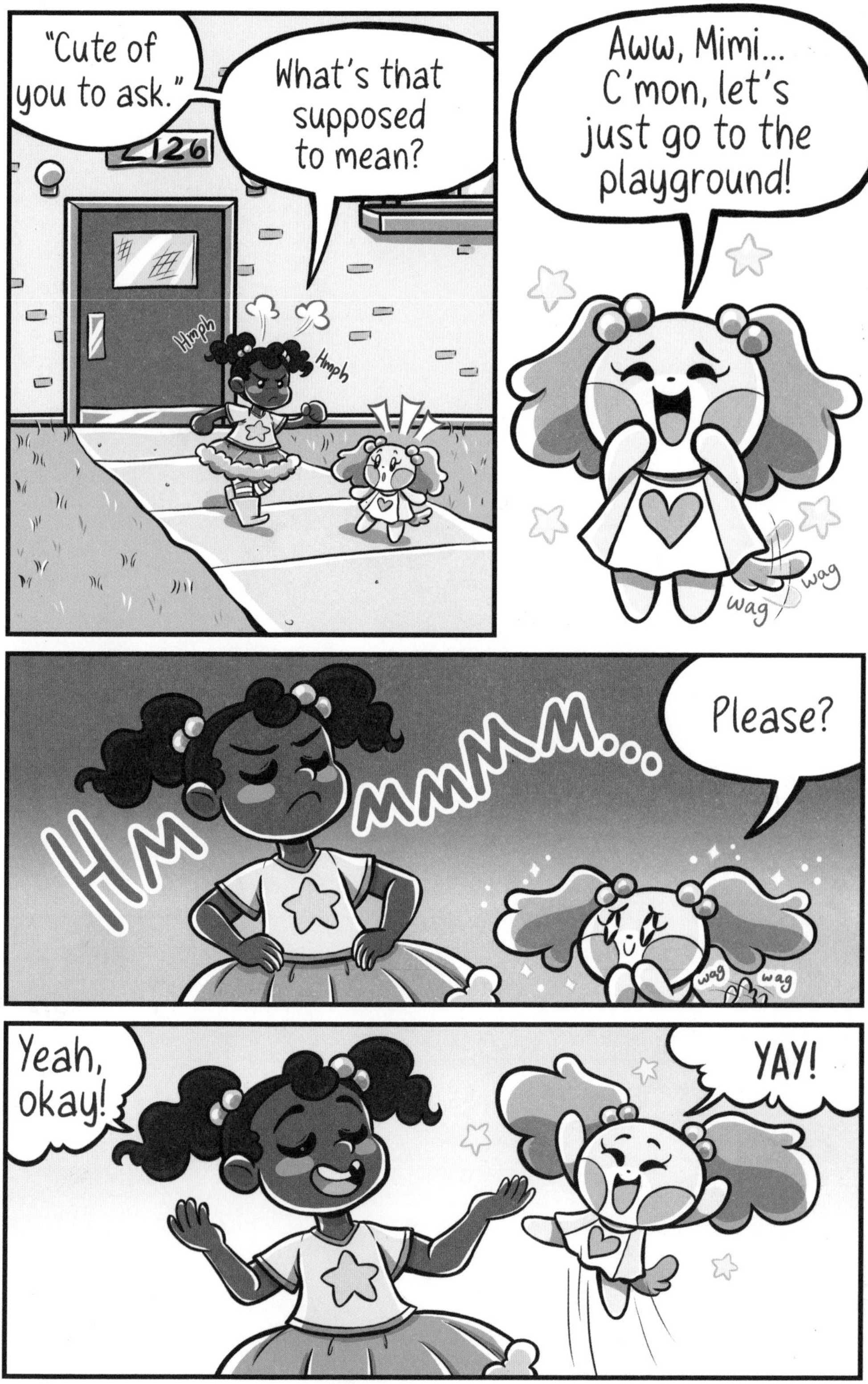
"Cute of you to ask."
What's that supposed to mean?
C126
Hmph
Hmph
Aww, Mimi... C'mon, let's just go to the playground!
wag wag
HMMMMM...
Please?
wag wag
Yeah, okay!
YAY!

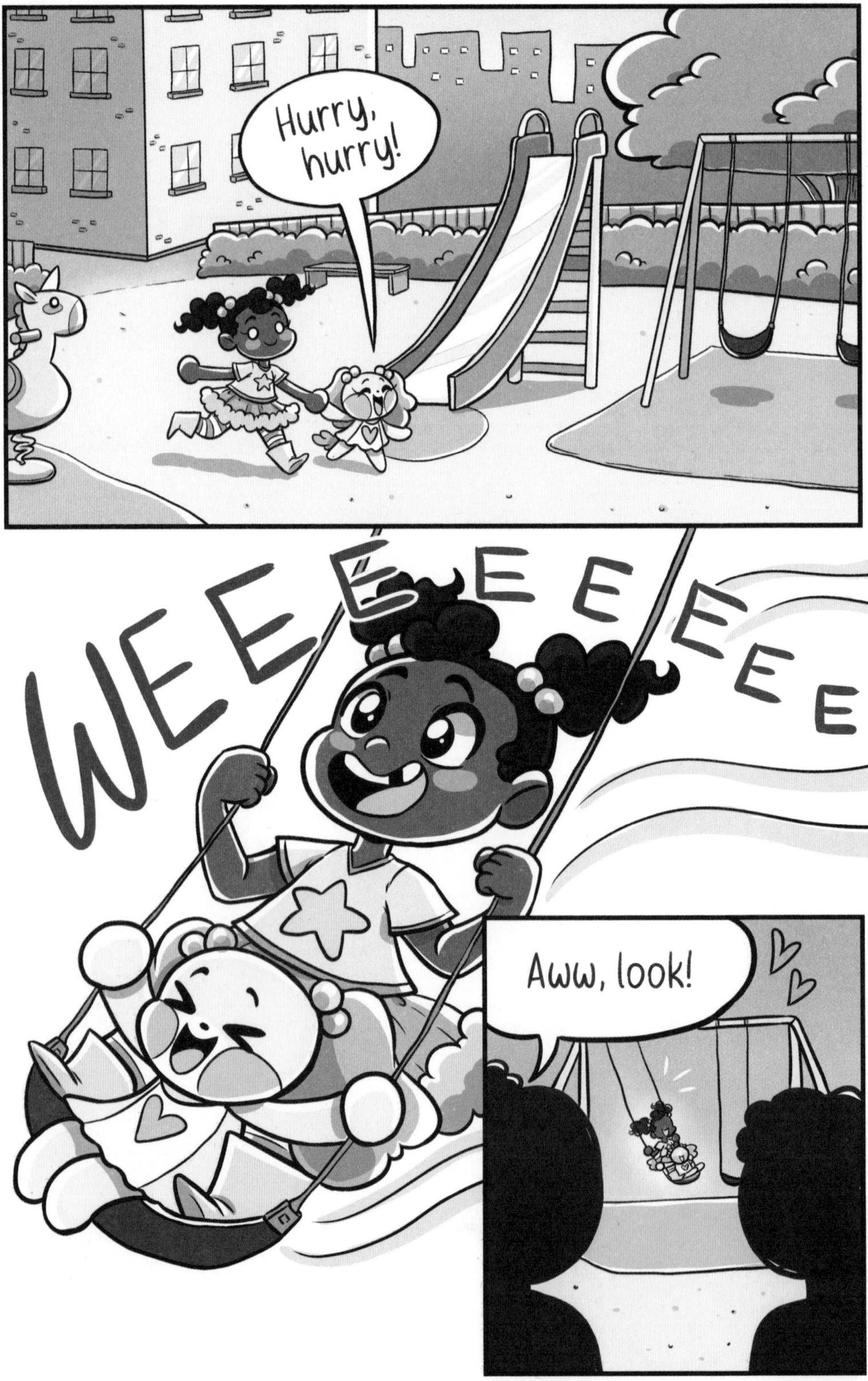
Hurry, hurry!
WEEEEEEEEE
Aww, look!

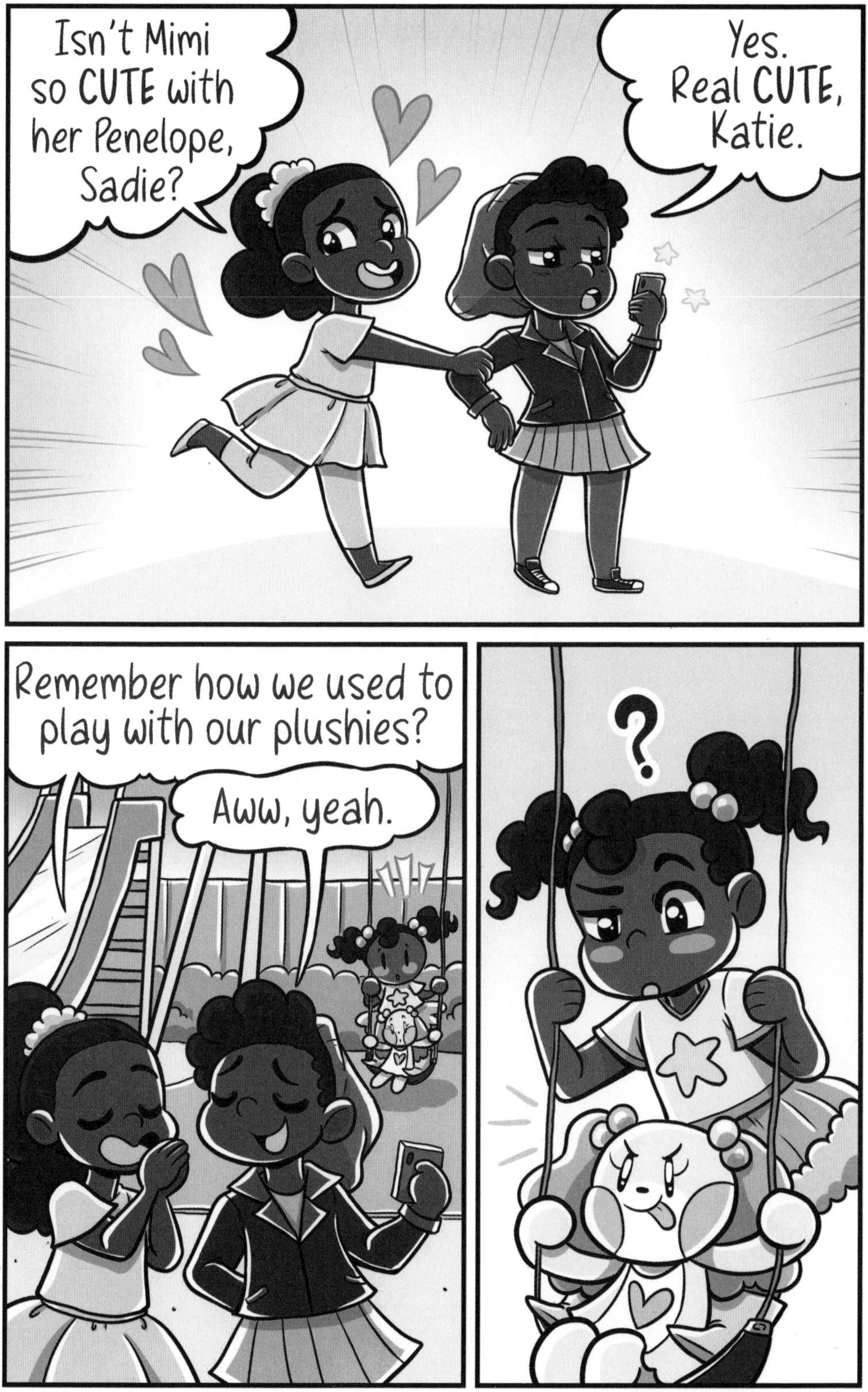
Isn't Mimi so CUTE with her Penelope, Sadie?
Yes. Real CUTE, Katie.
Remember how we used to play with our plushies?
Aww, yeah.
?

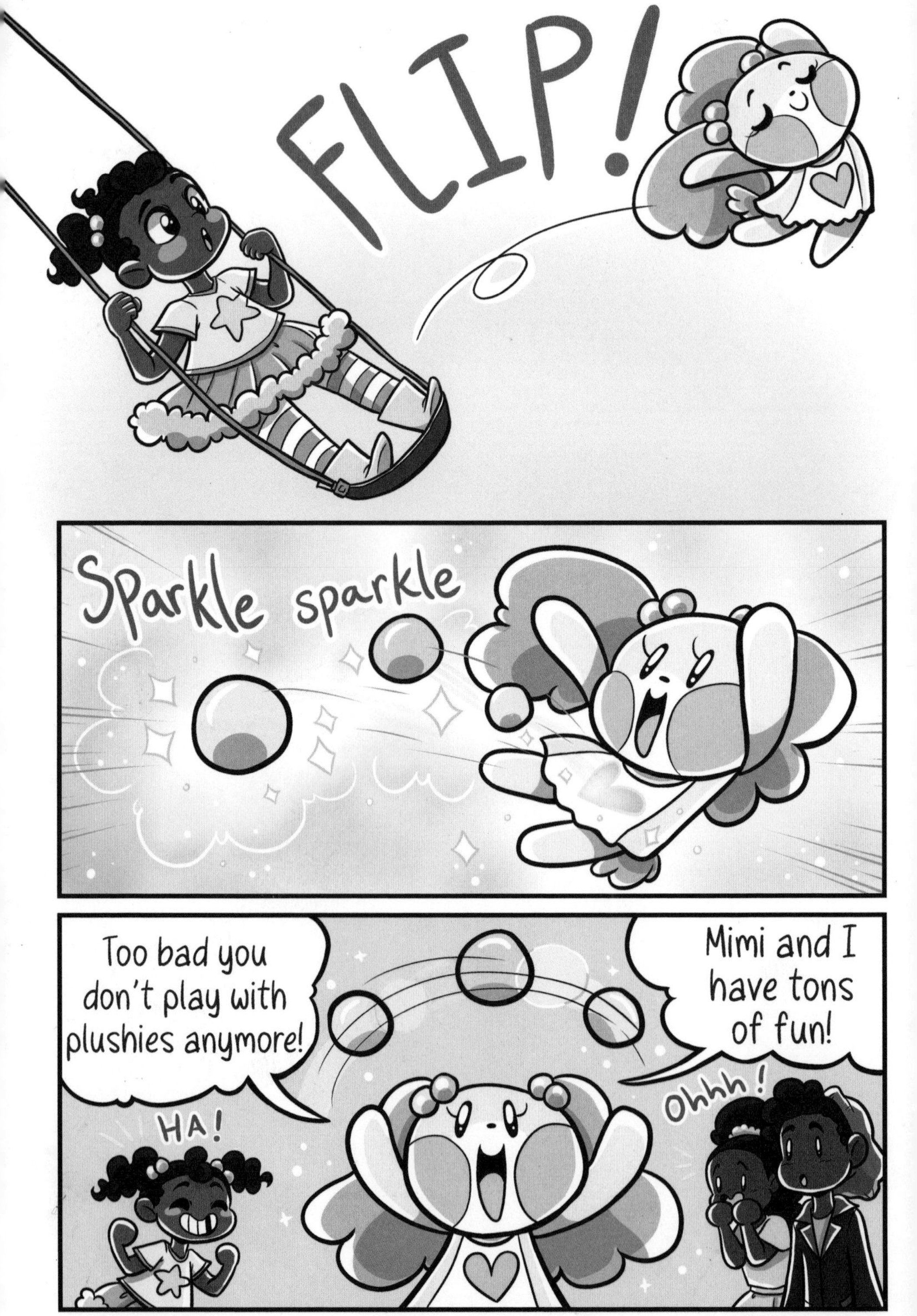
FLIP!
Sparkle sparkle
Too bad you don't play with plushies anymore!
Mimi and I have tons of fun!
HA!
Ohhh!

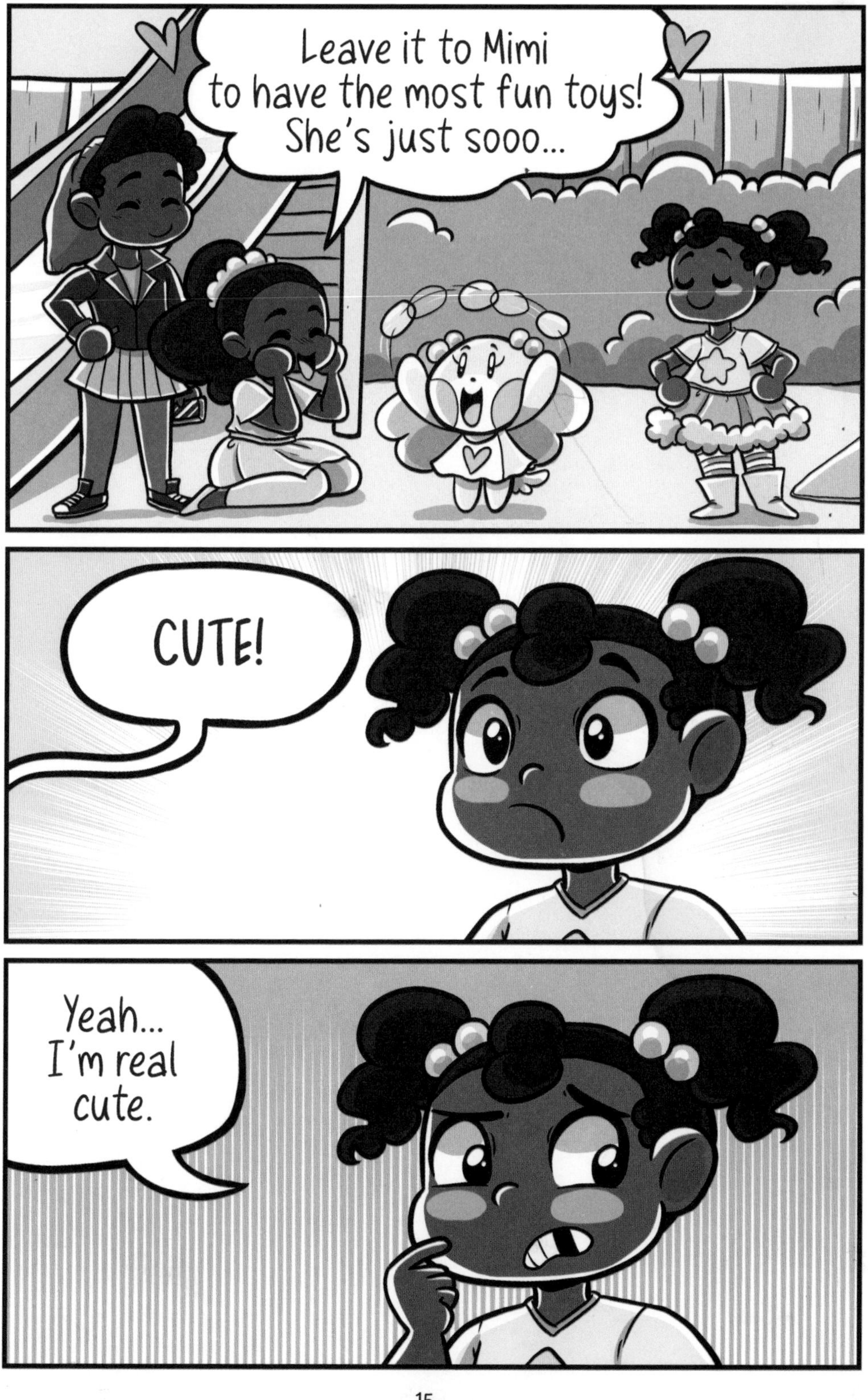
Leave it to Mimi to have the most fun toys! She's just sooo...
CUTE!
Yeah... I'm real cute.

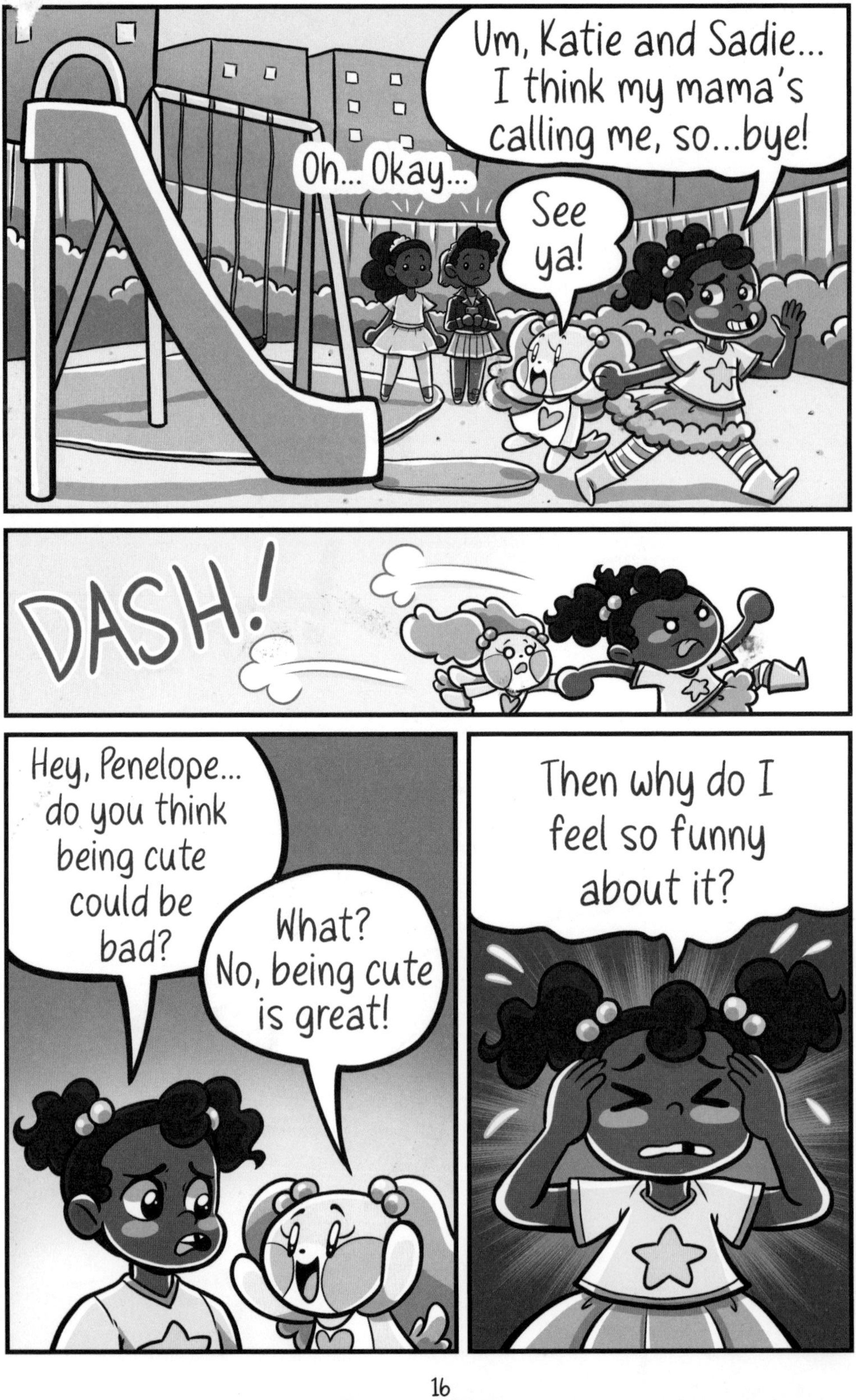
Um, Katie and Sadie... I think my mama's calling me, so...bye!
Oh... Okay...
See ya!
DASH!
Hey, Penelope... do you think being cute could be bad?
What? No, being cute is great!
Then why do I feel so funny about it?

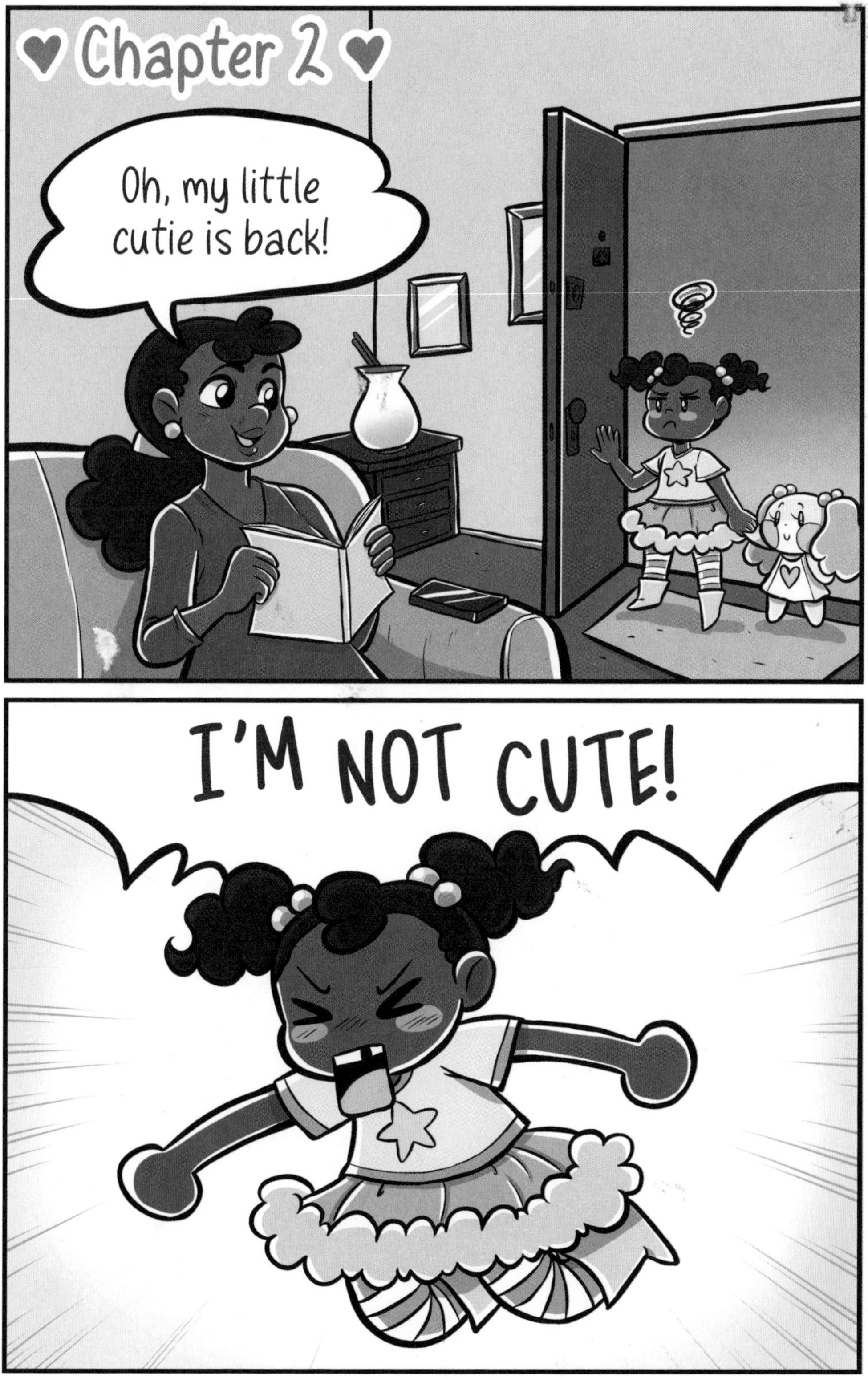
♥ Chapter 2 ♥
Oh, my little cutie is back!
I'M NOT CUTE!

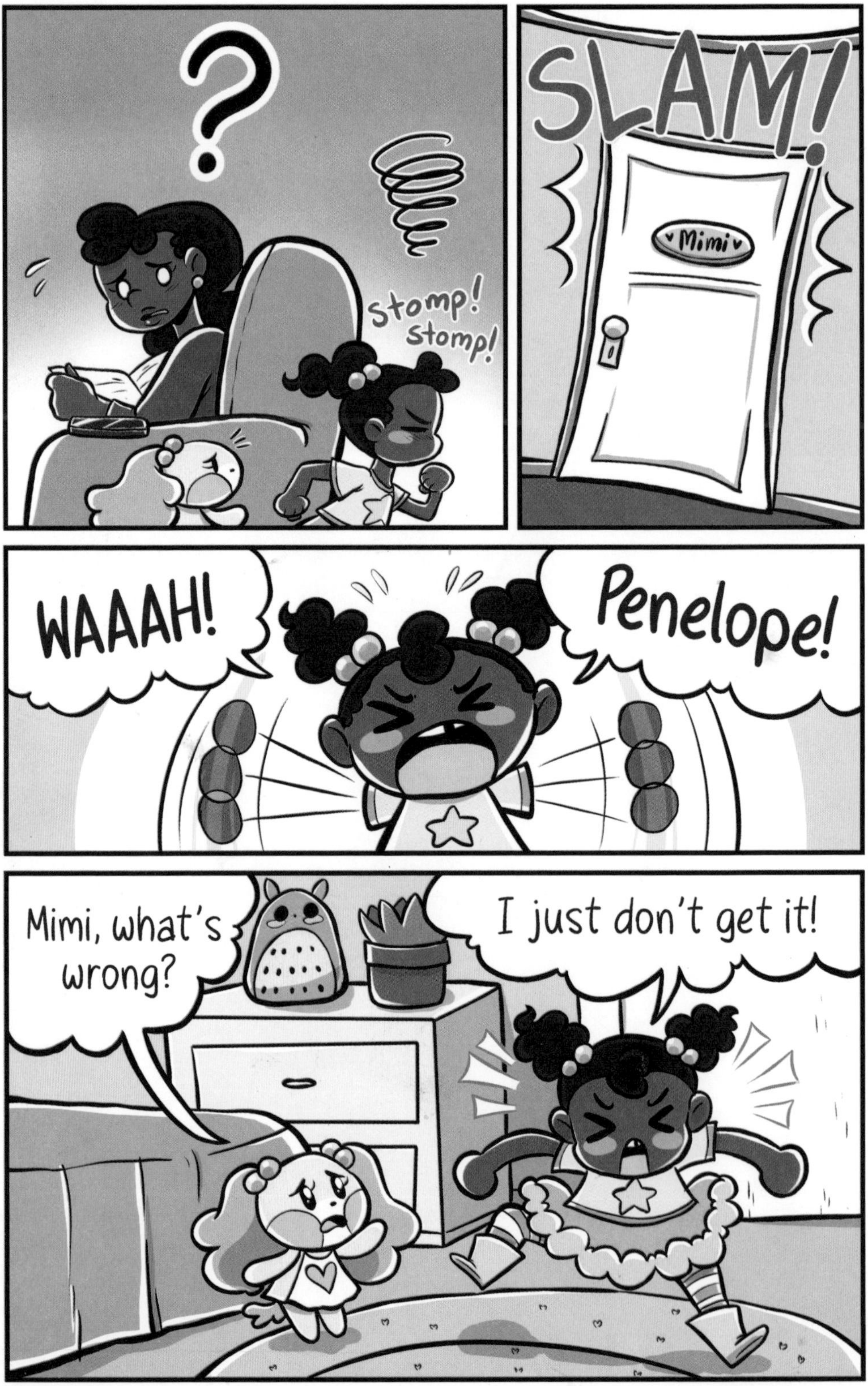
?
Stomp! Stomp!
SLAM!
Mimi
WAAAH!
Penelope!
Mimi, what's wrong?
I just don't get it!

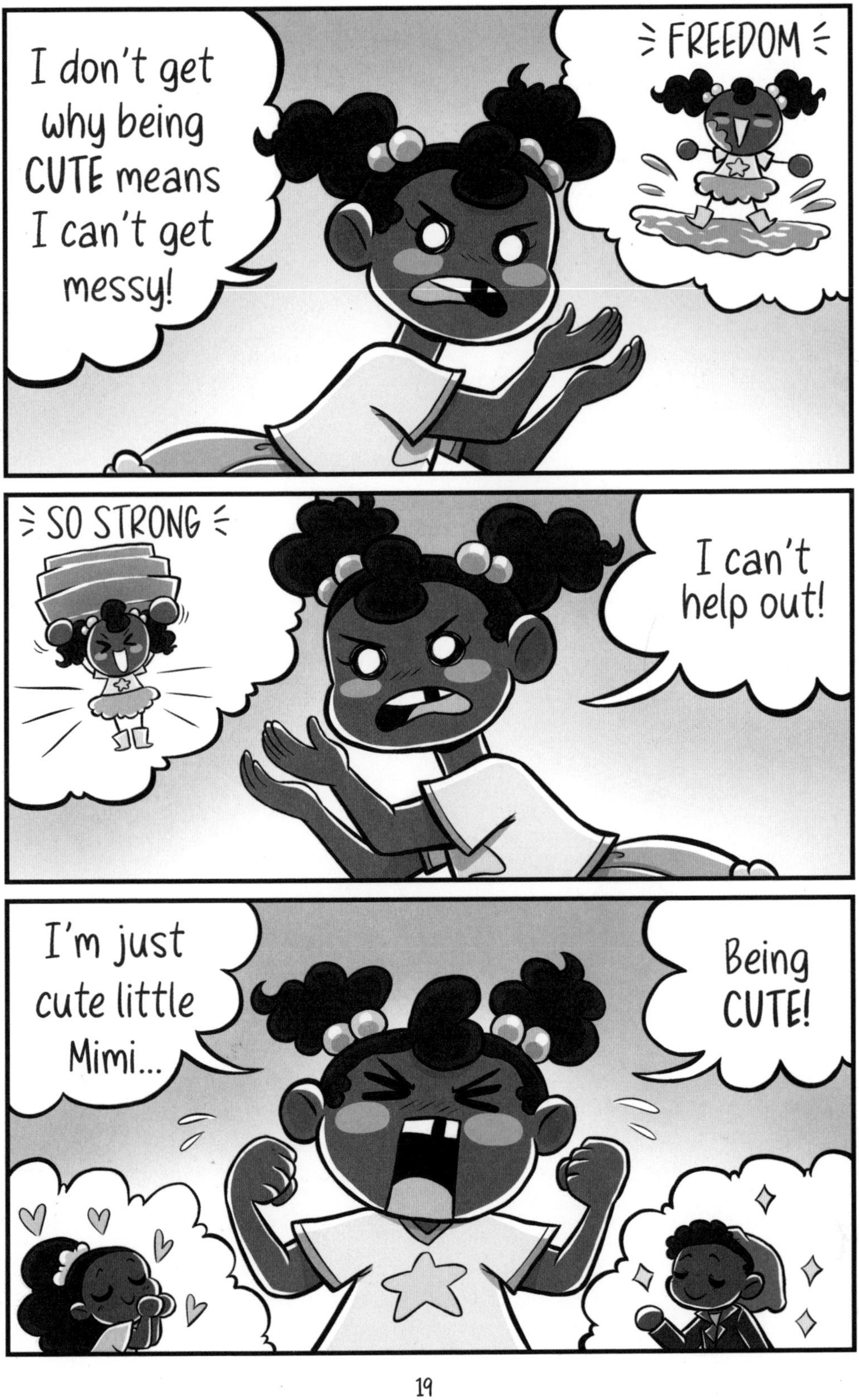
I don't get why being CUTE means I can't get messy!
FREEDOM
SO STRONG
I can't help out!
I'm just cute little Mimi...
Being CUTE!

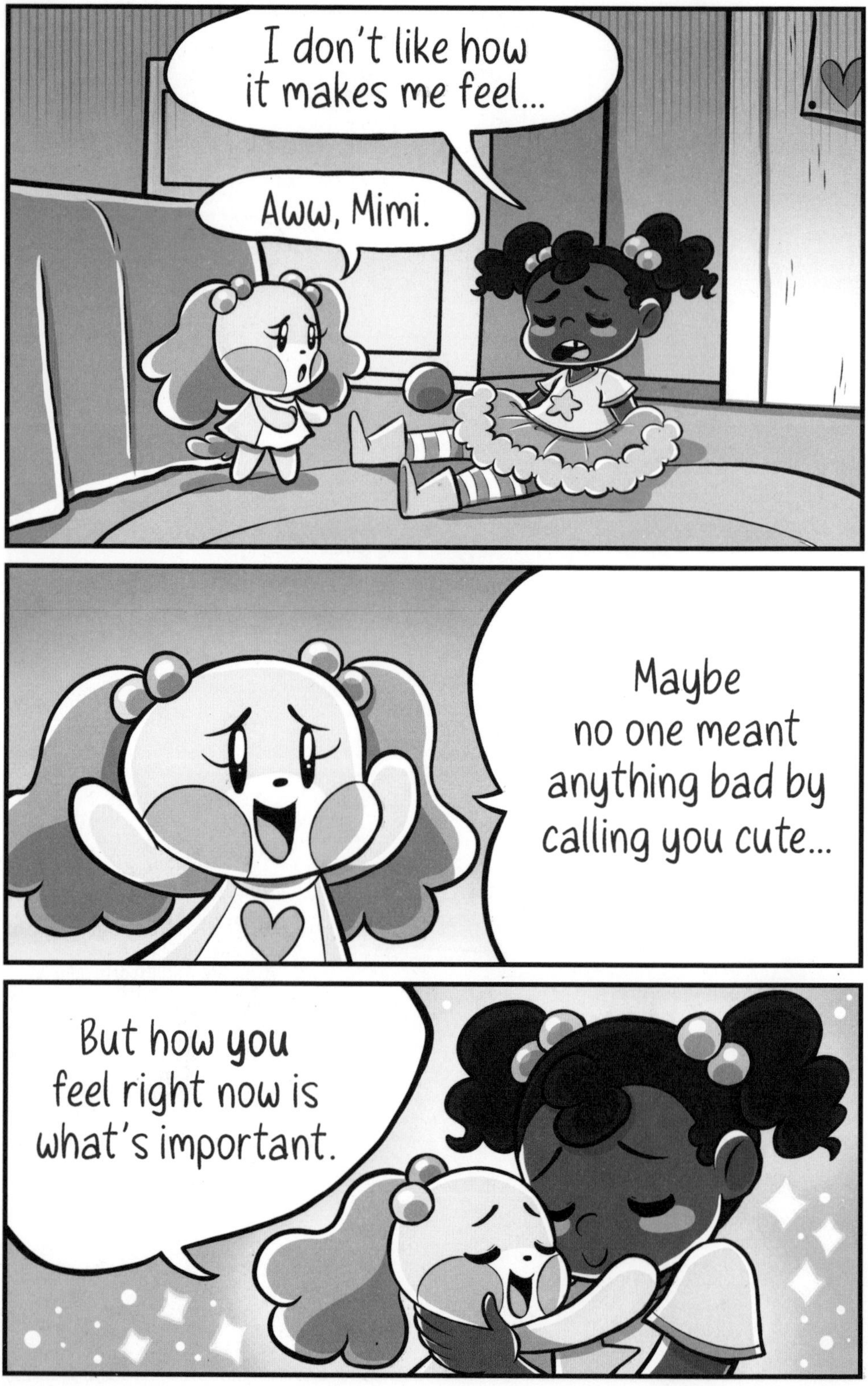
I don't like how it makes me feel...
Aww, Mimi.
Maybe no one meant anything bad by calling you cute...
But how you feel right now is what's important.

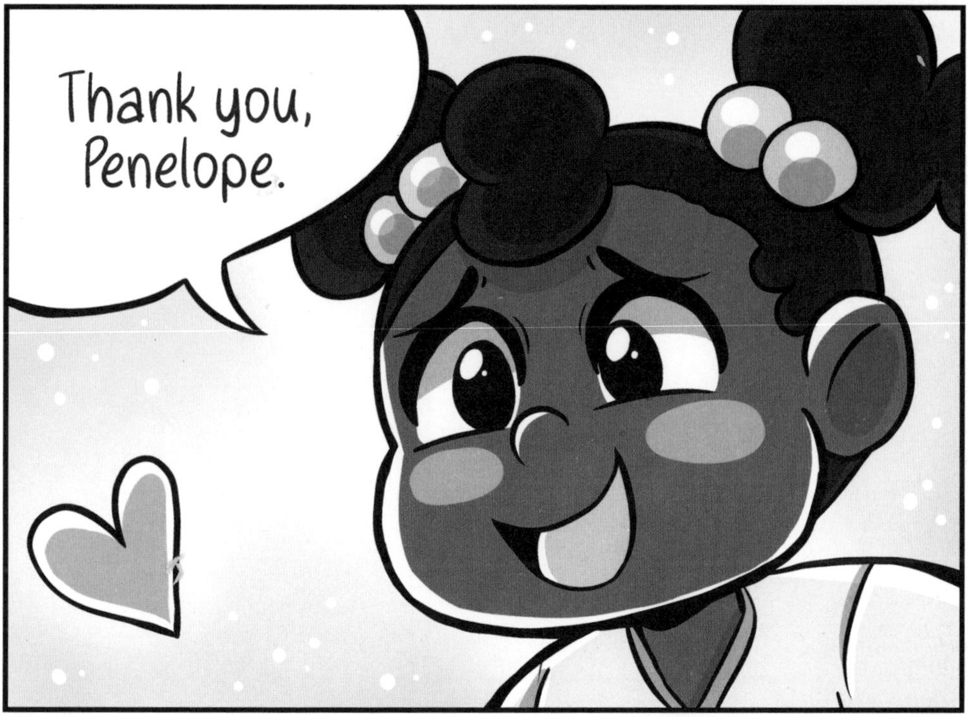
Thank you, Penelope.

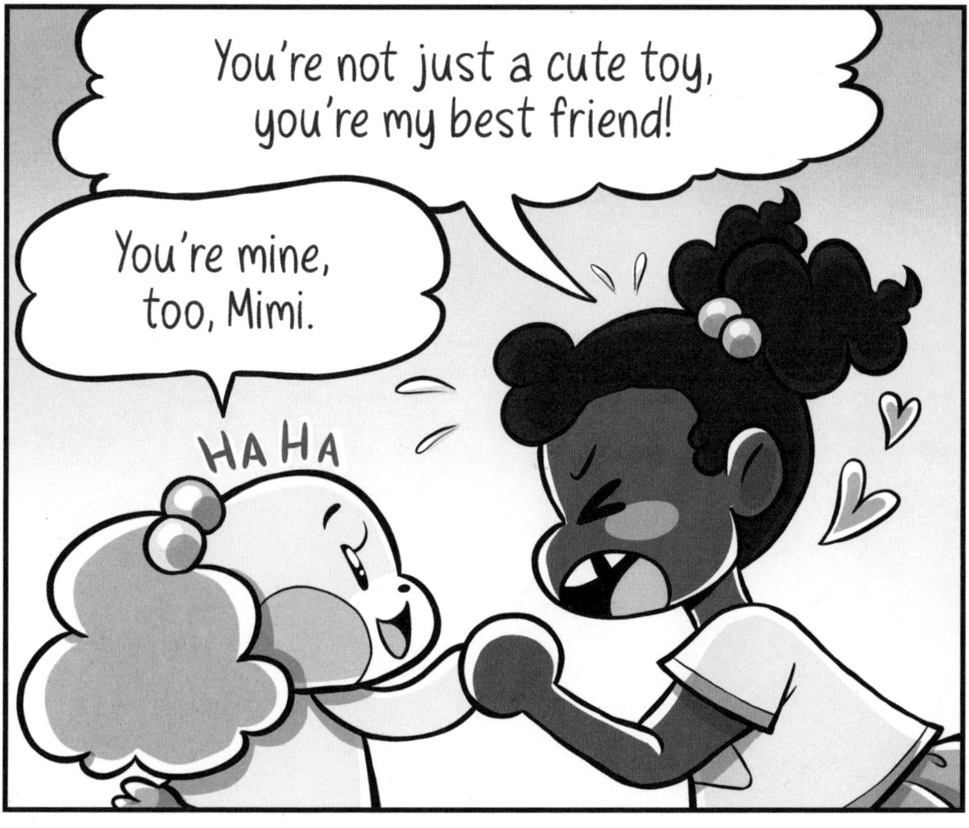
You're not just a cute toy, you're my best friend!
You're mine, too, Mimi.
HA HA

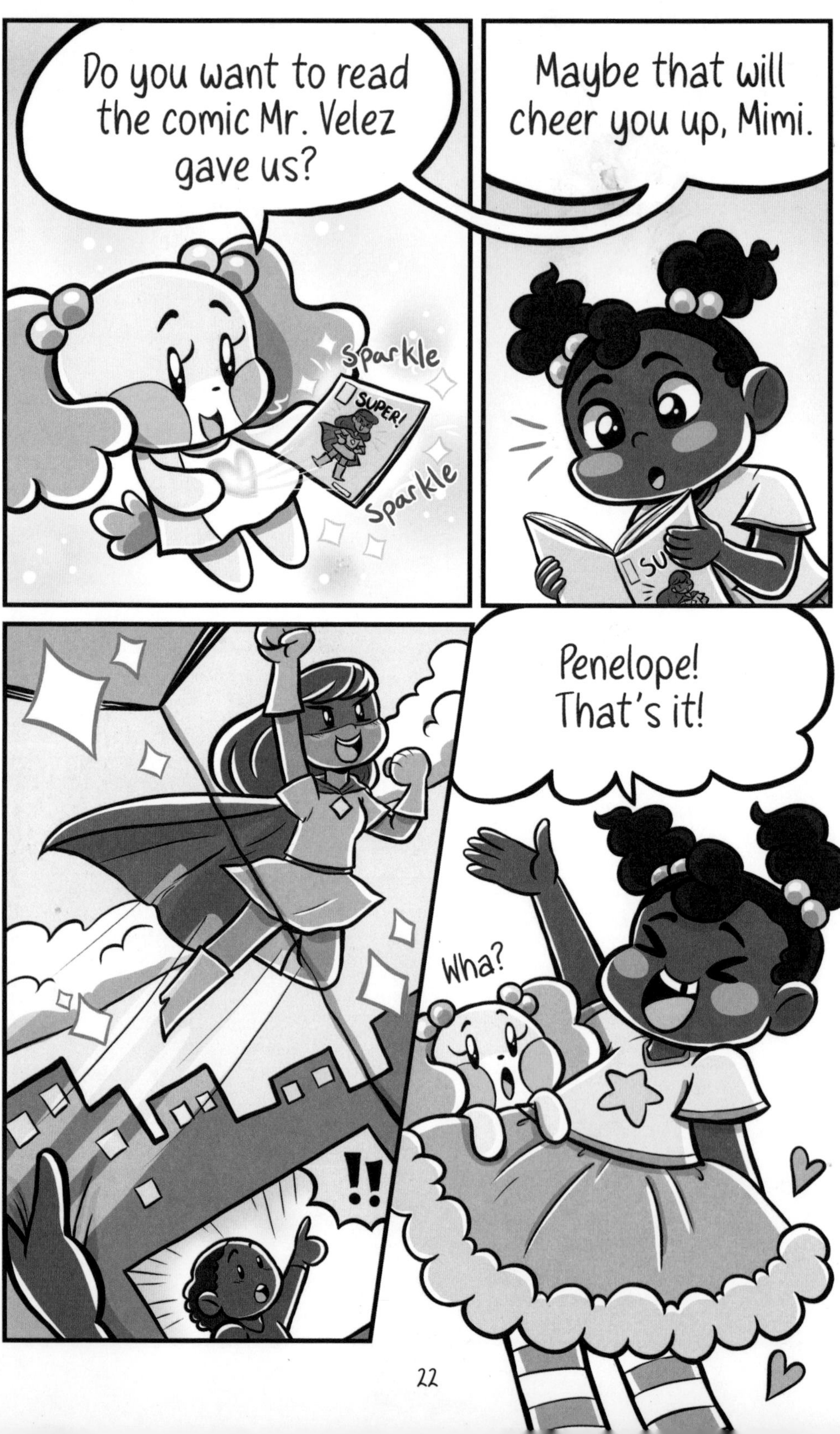

Do you want to read the comic Mr. Velez gave us?
Sparkle
SUPER!
Sparkle
Maybe that will cheer you up, Mimi.
SU
!!
Penelope! That's it!
Wha?

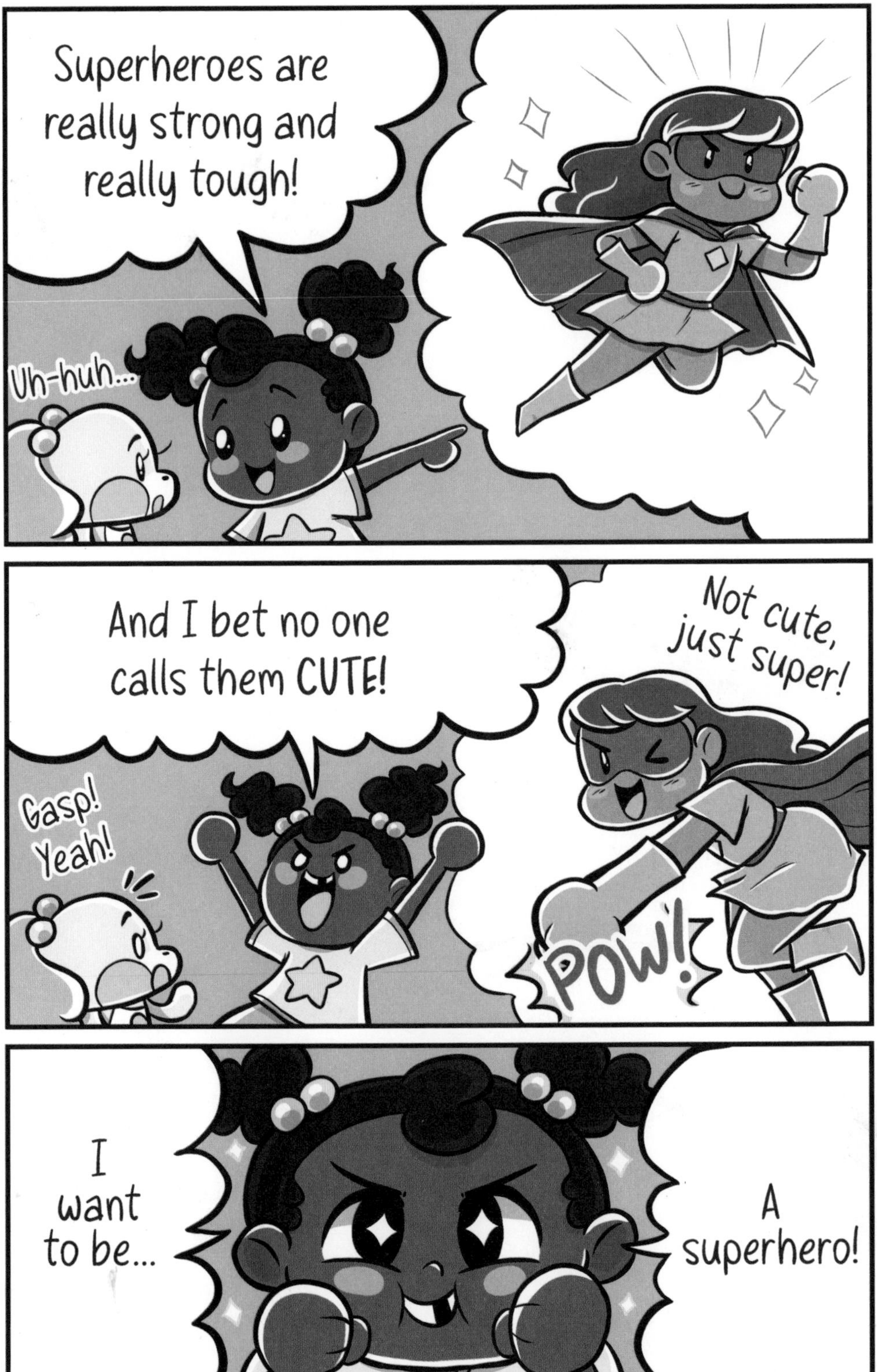
Superheroes are really strong and really tough!
Uh-huh...
And I bet no one calls them CUTE!
Not cute, just super!
Gasp! Yeah!
POW!
I want to be...
A superhero!

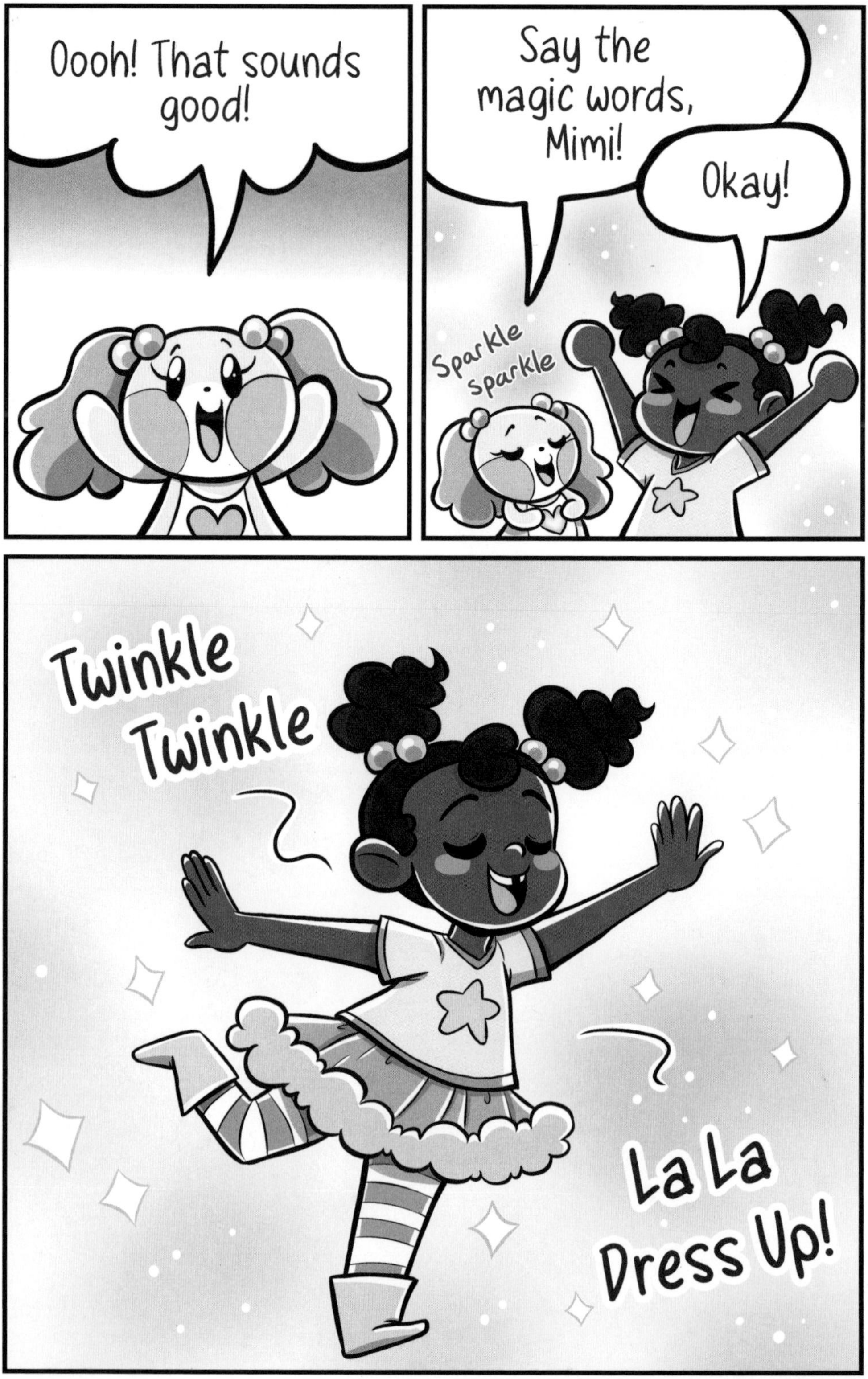

Oooh! That sounds good!
Say the magic words, Mimi!
Okay!
Sparkle sparkle
Twinkle Twinkle
La La Dress Up!

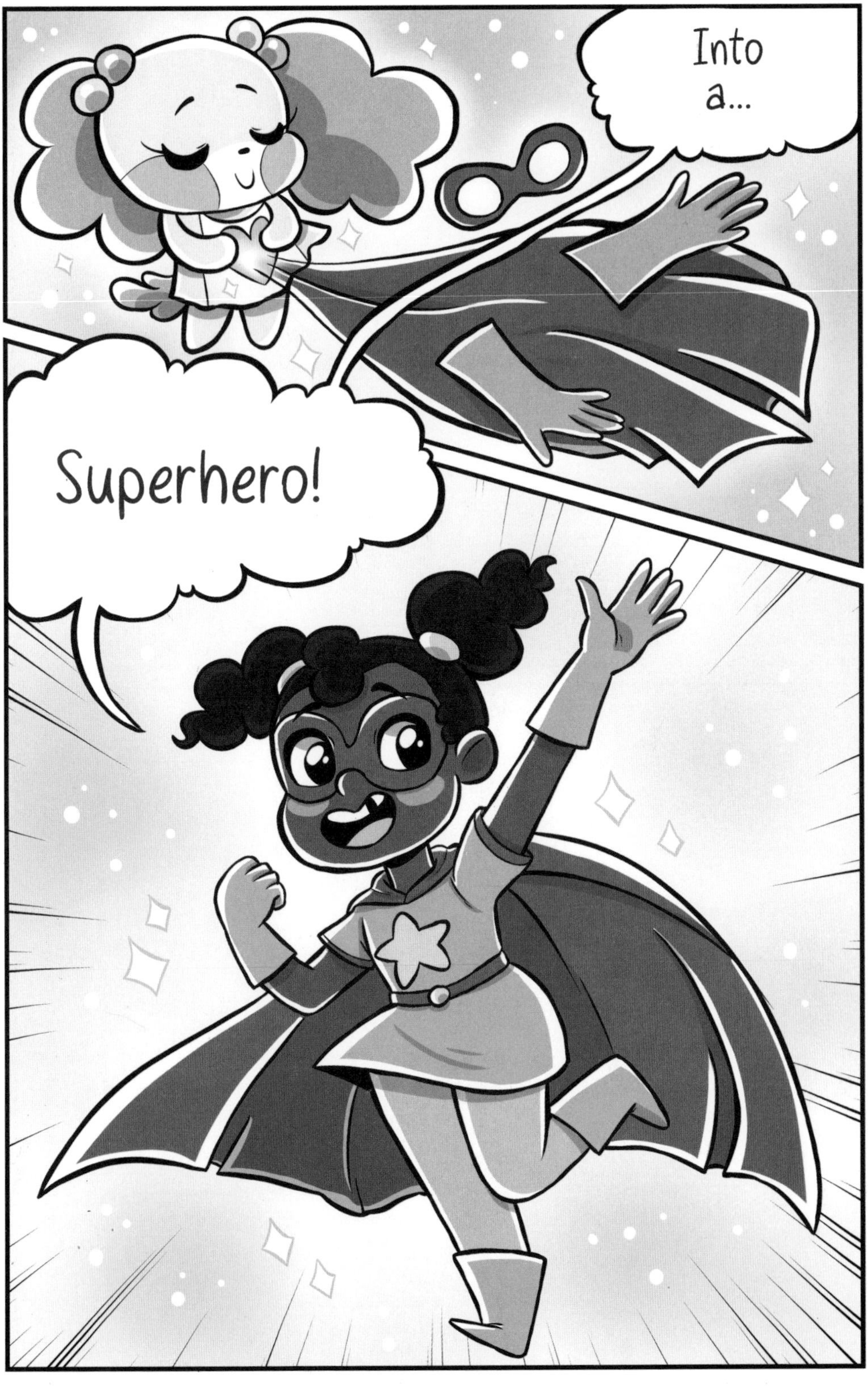
Into a...
Superhero!

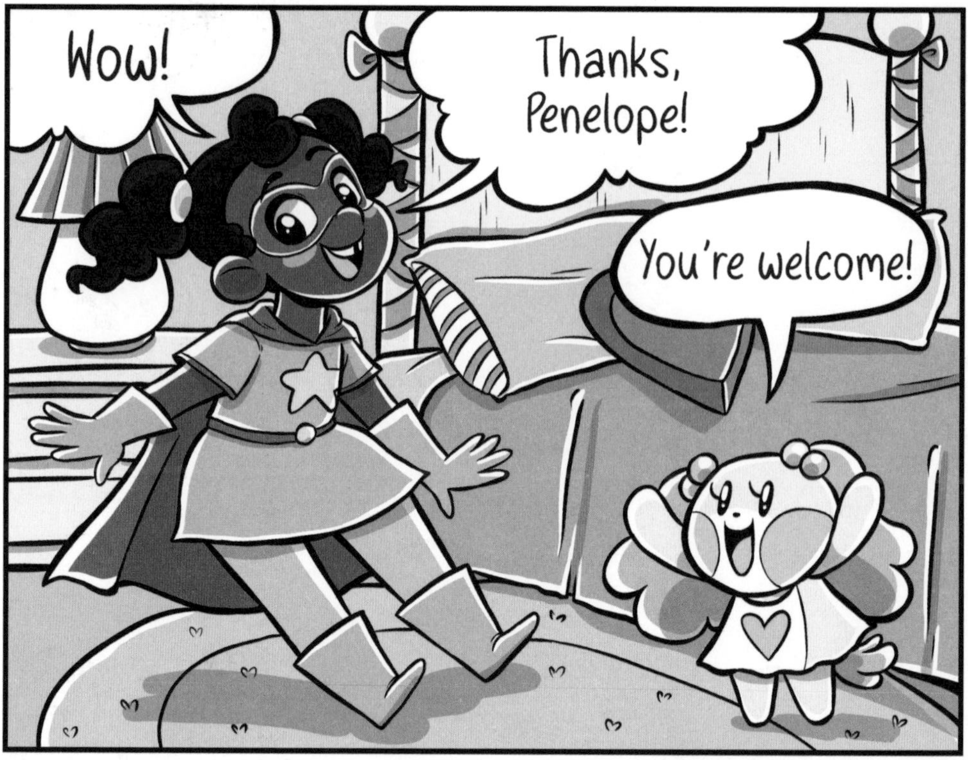
Wow!
Thanks, Penelope!
You're welcome!

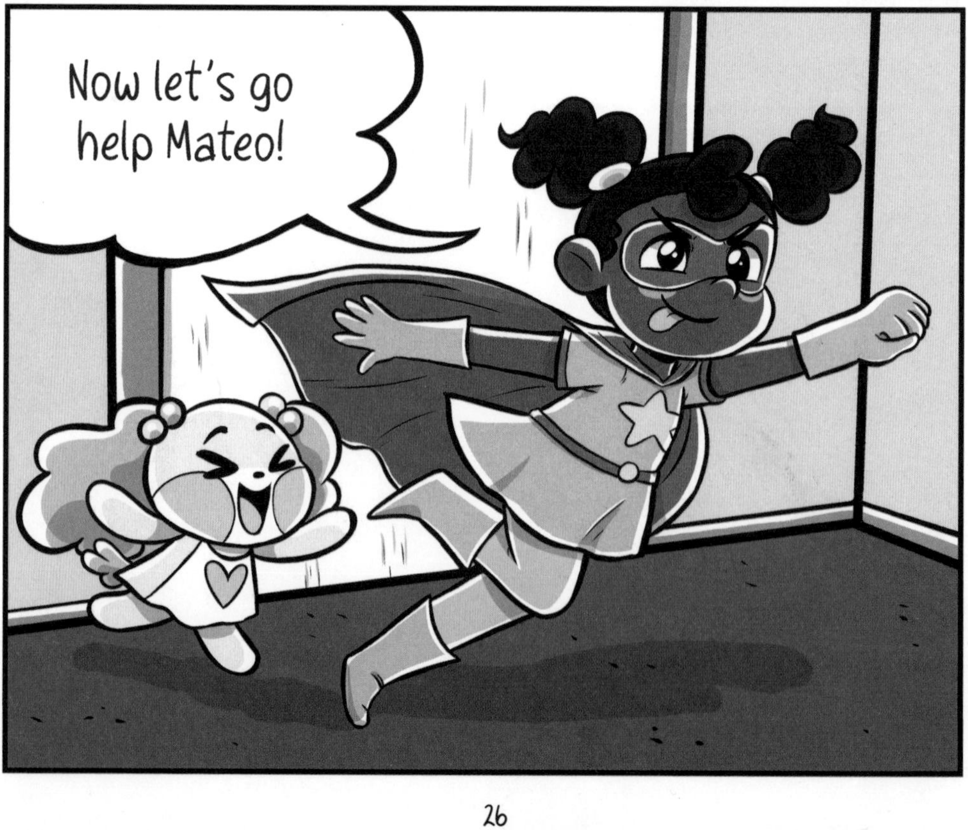
Now let's go help Mateo!

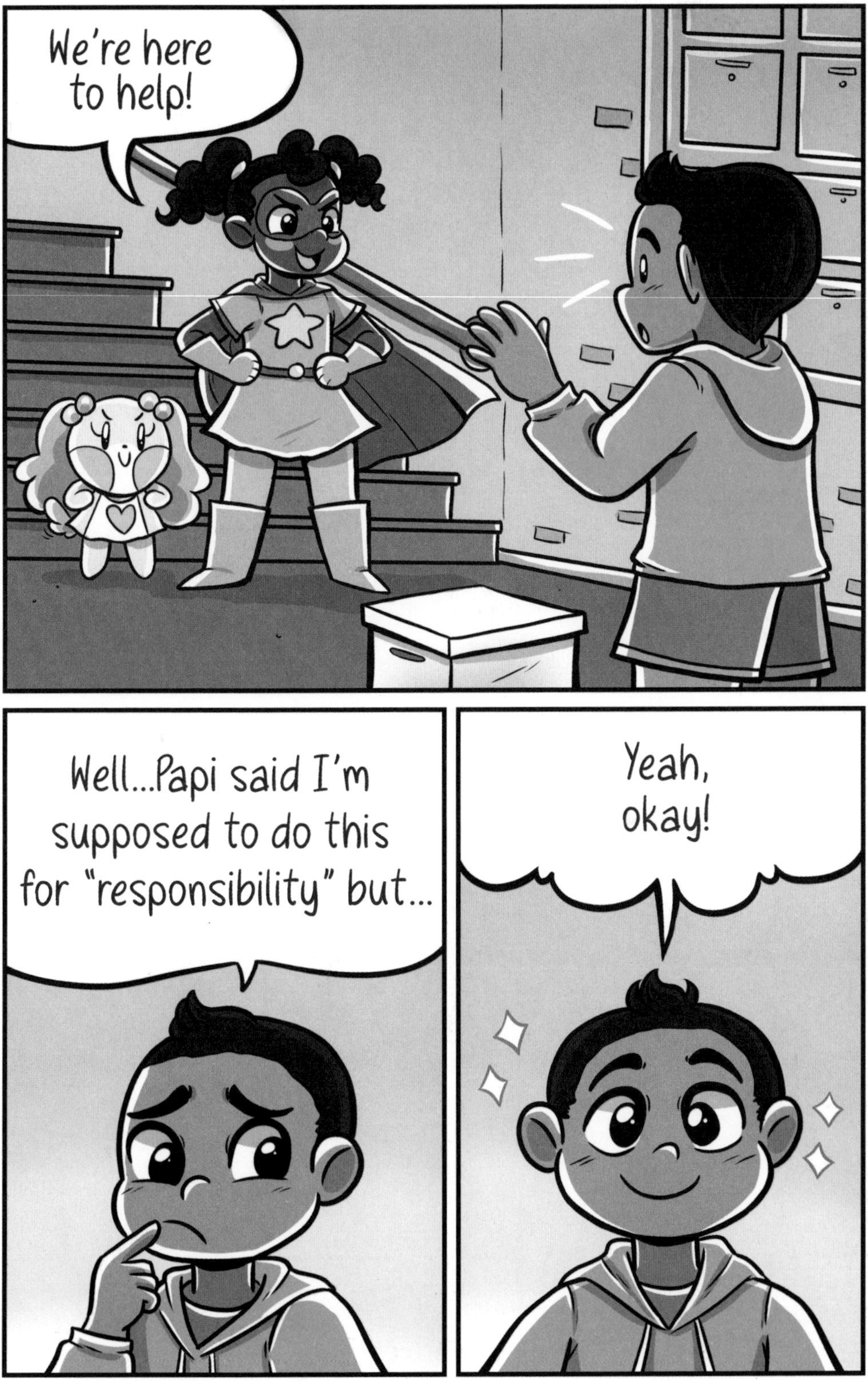
We're here to help!
Well...Papi said I'm supposed to do this for "responsibility" but...
Yeah, okay!

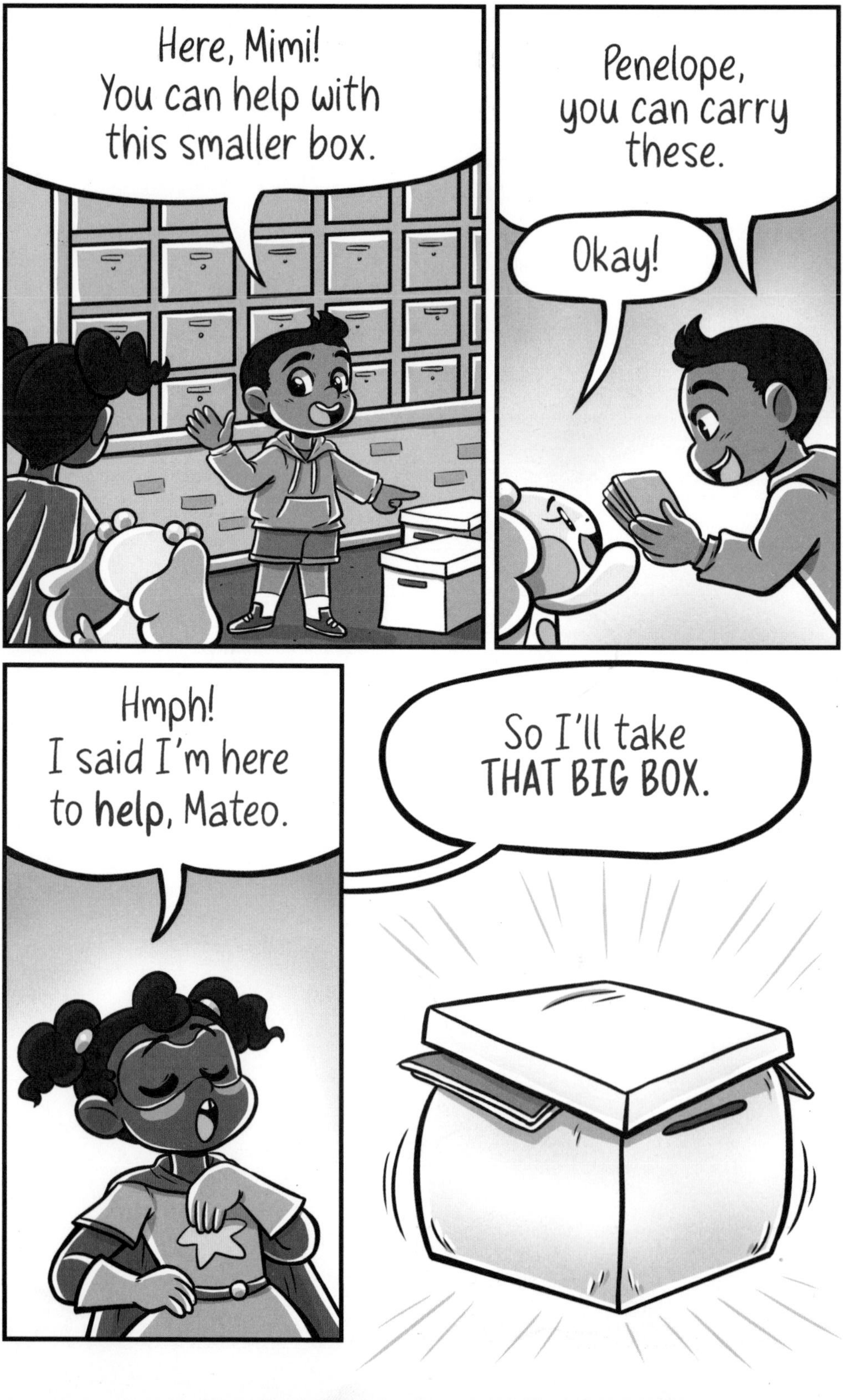
Here, Mimi! You can help with this smaller box.
Penelope, you can carry these.
Okay!
Hmph! I said I'm here to **help**, Mateo.
So I'll take **THAT BIG BOX.**

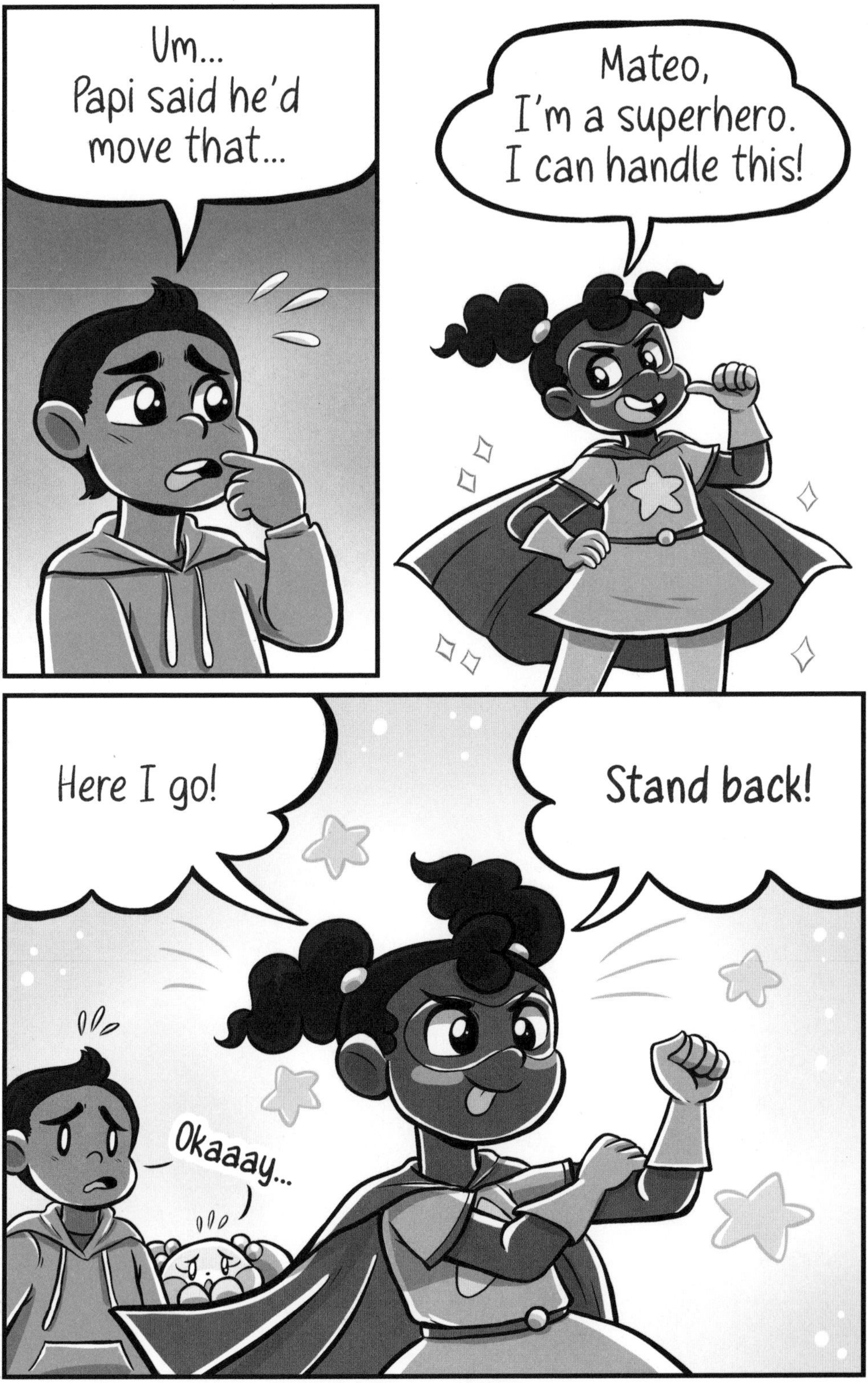
Um...
Papi said he'd move that...
Mateo,
I'm a superhero.
I can handle this!
Here I go!
Stand back!
Okaaay...

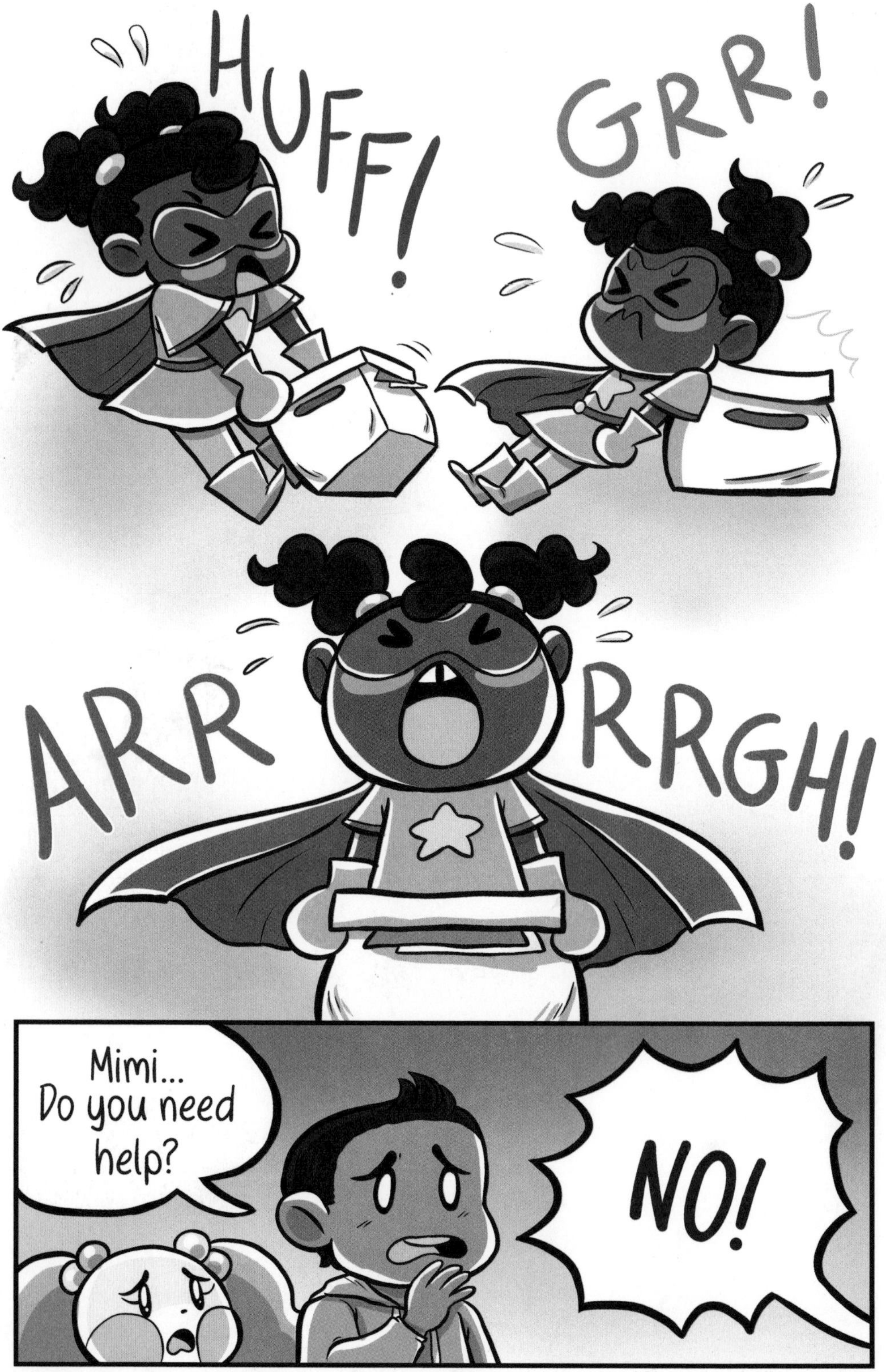
HUFF!
GRR!
ARRRRGH!
Mimi... Do you need help?
NO!

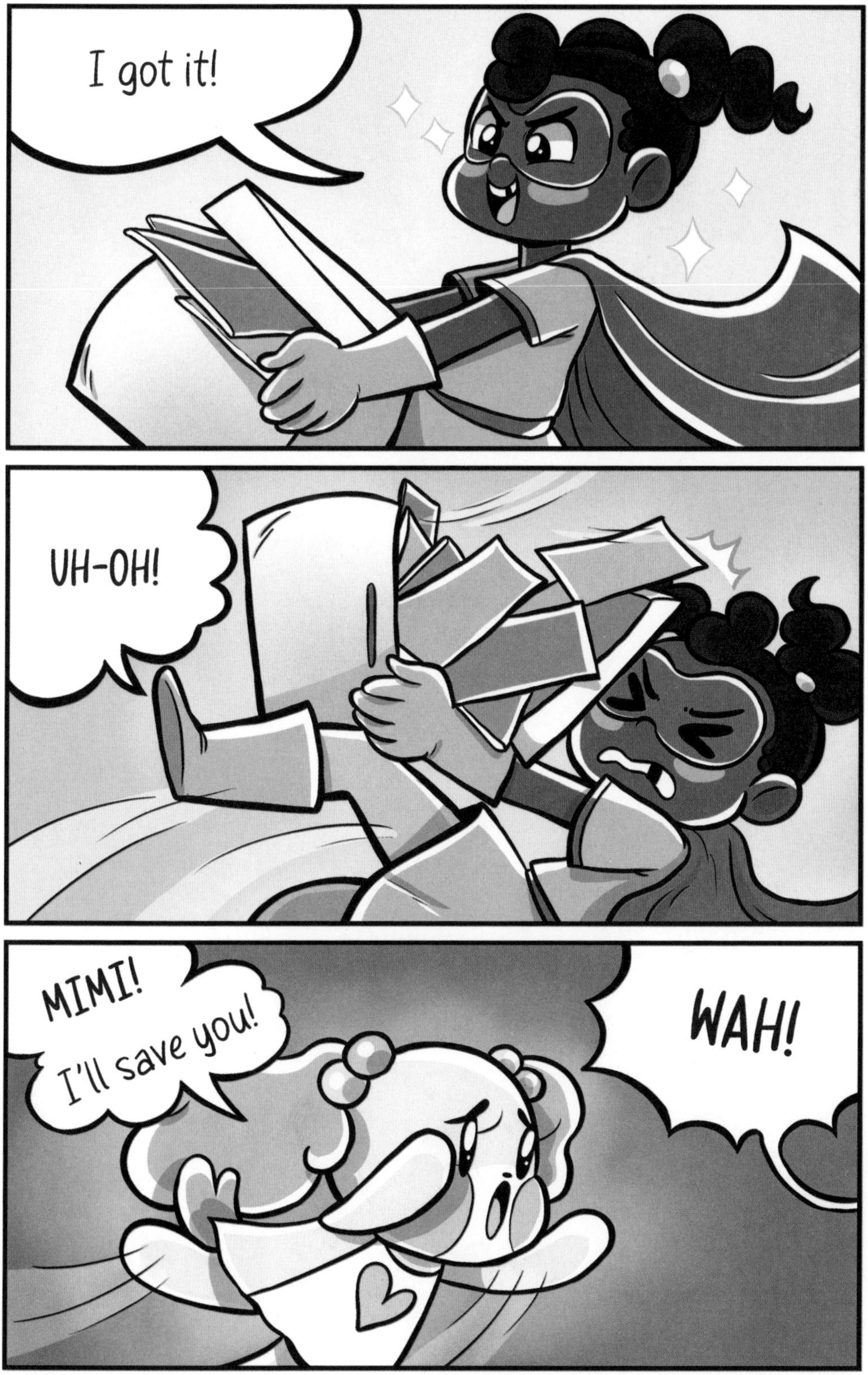
I got it!
UH-OH!
MIMI! I'll save you!
WAH!

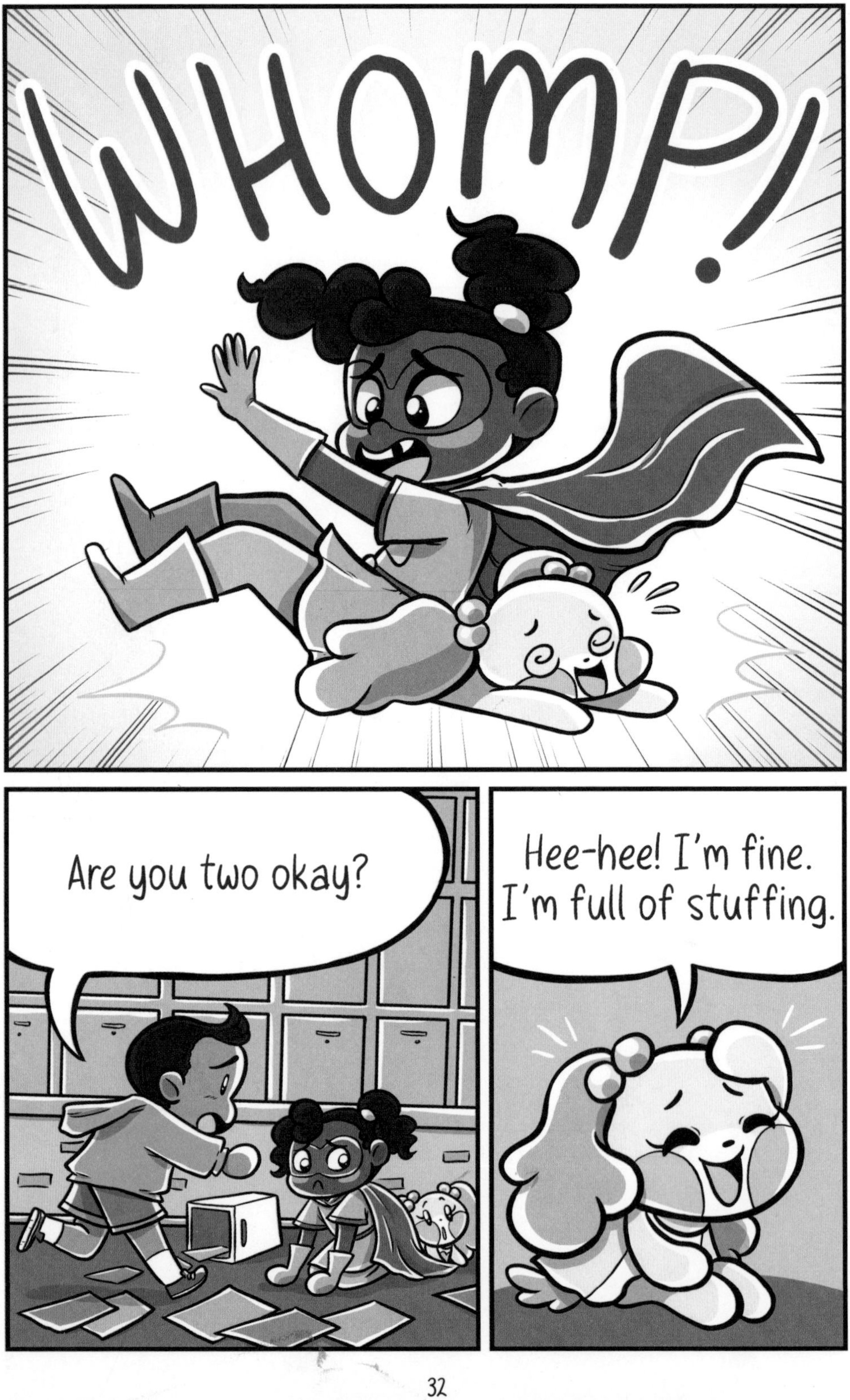
WHOMP!
Are you two okay?
Hee-hee! I'm fine. I'm full of stuffing.

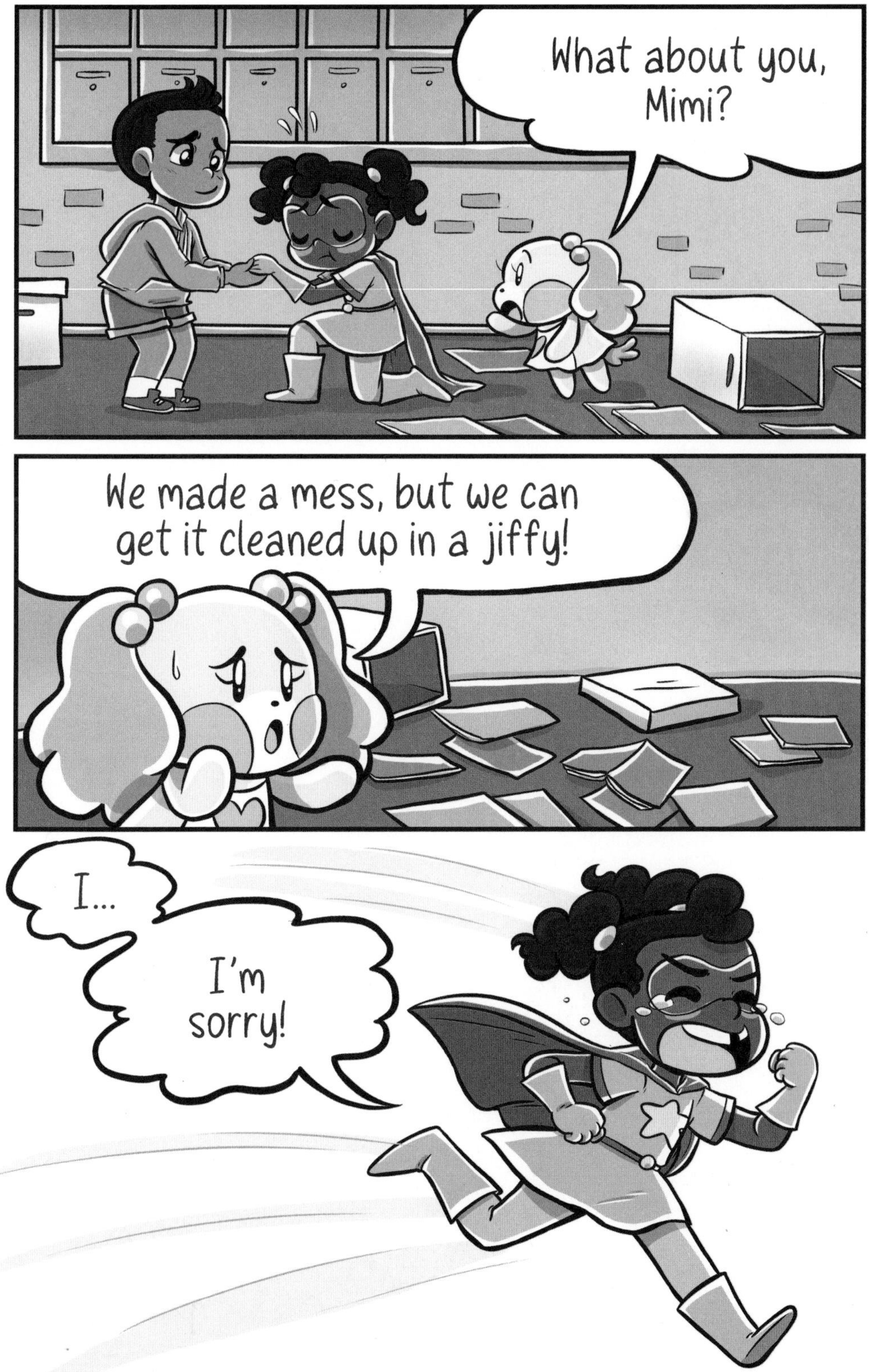
What about you, Mimi?
We made a mess, but we can get it cleaned up in a jiffy!
I...
I'm sorry!

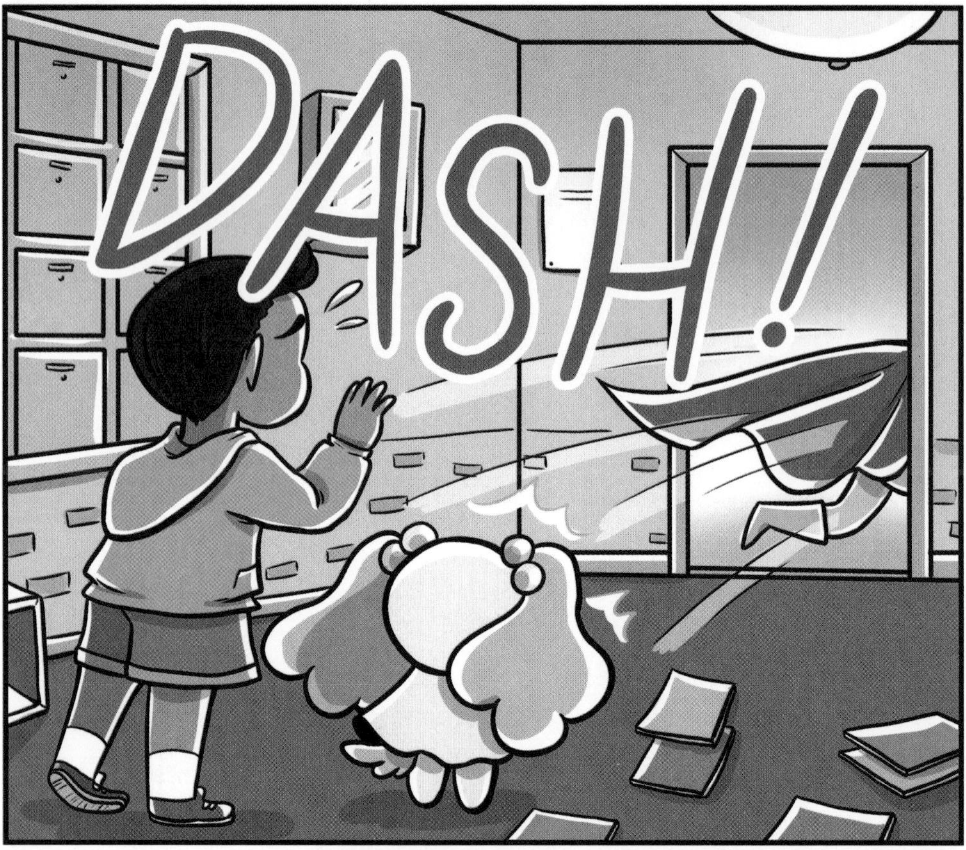
DASH!

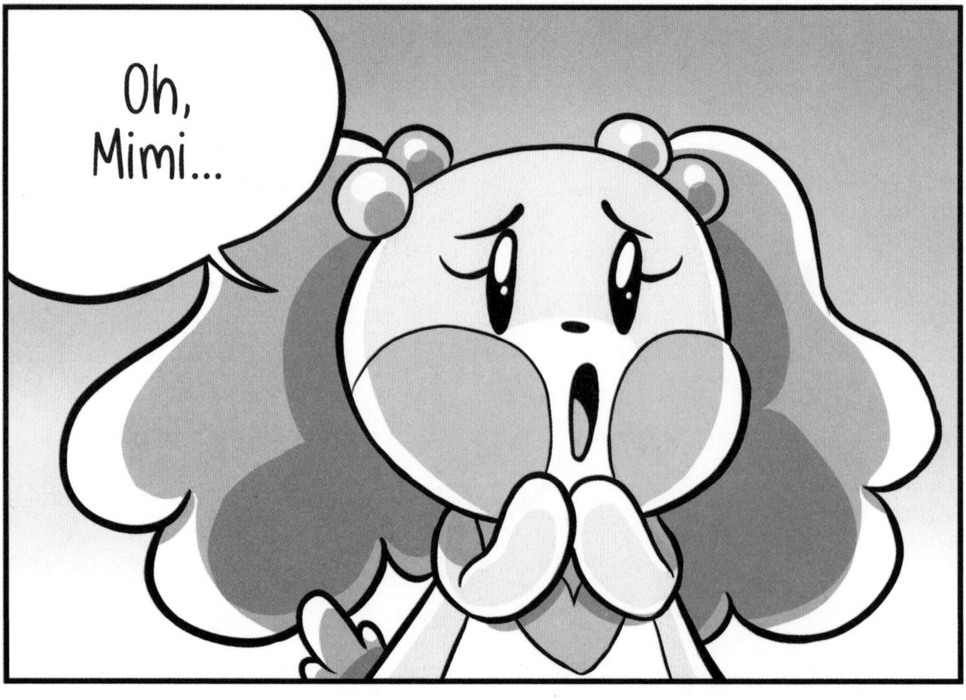
Oh, Mimi...

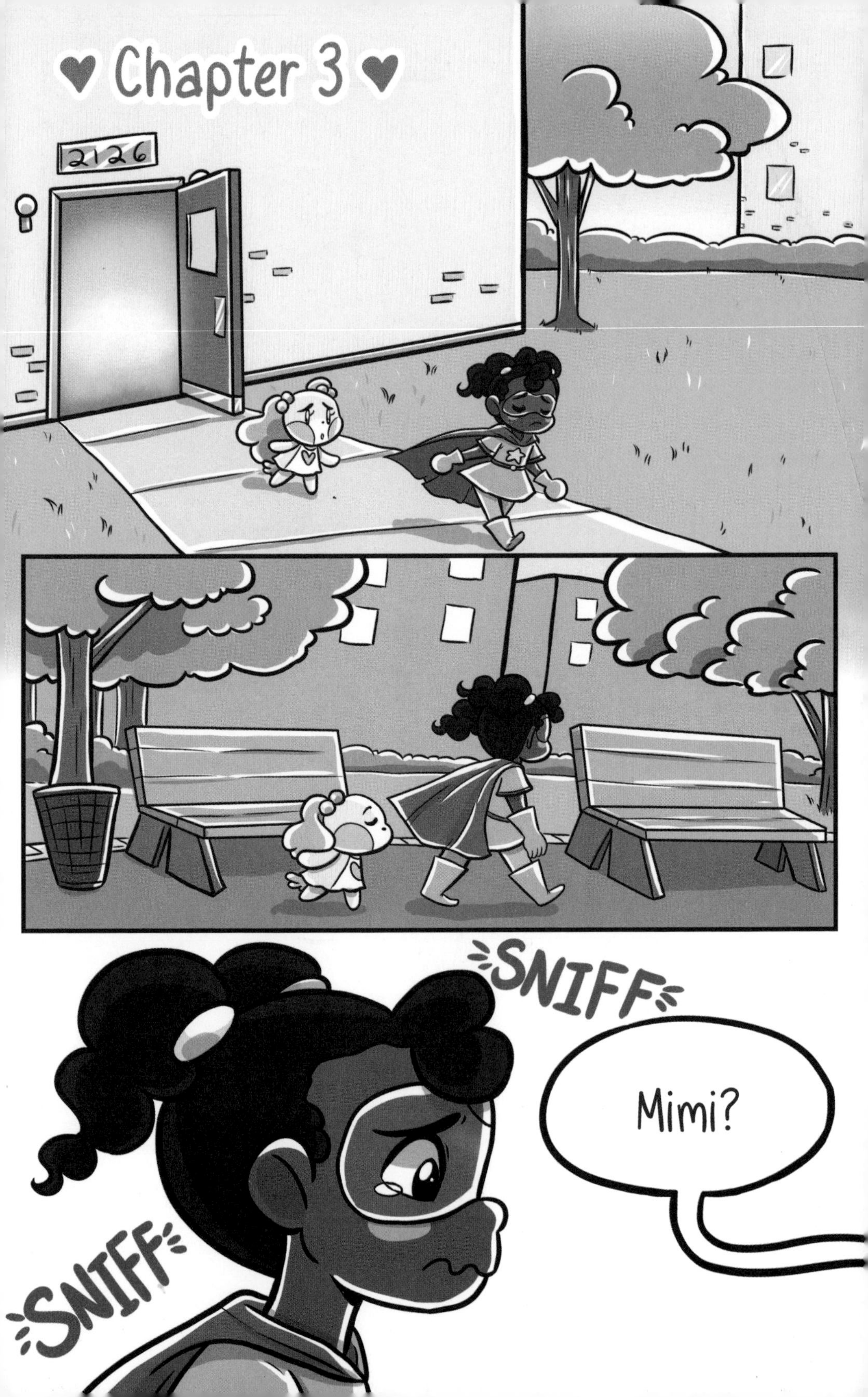
♥ Chapter 3 ♥
2126
SNIFF
SNIFF
Mimi?

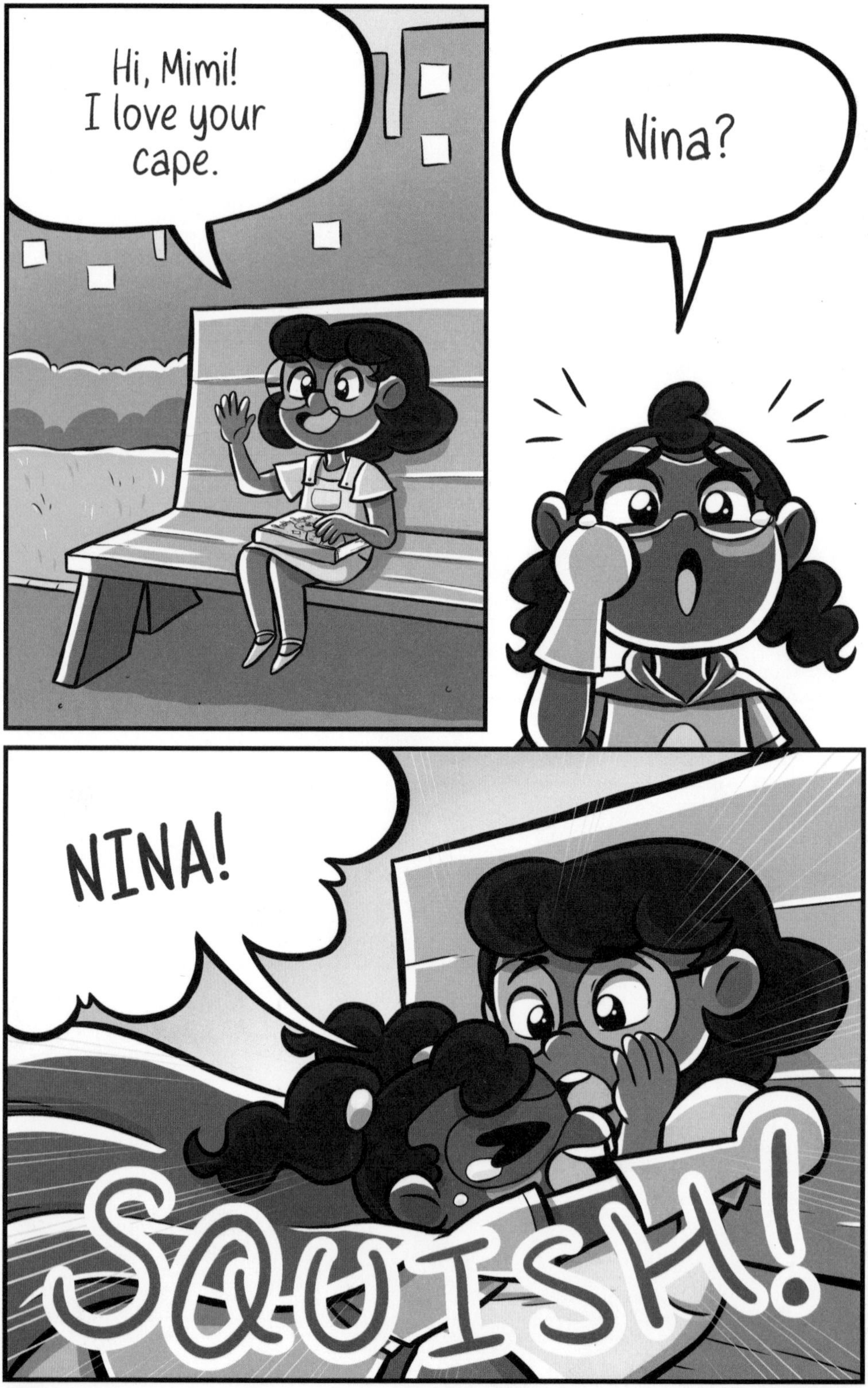
Hi, Mimi!
I love your
cape.
Nina?
NINA!
SQUISH!

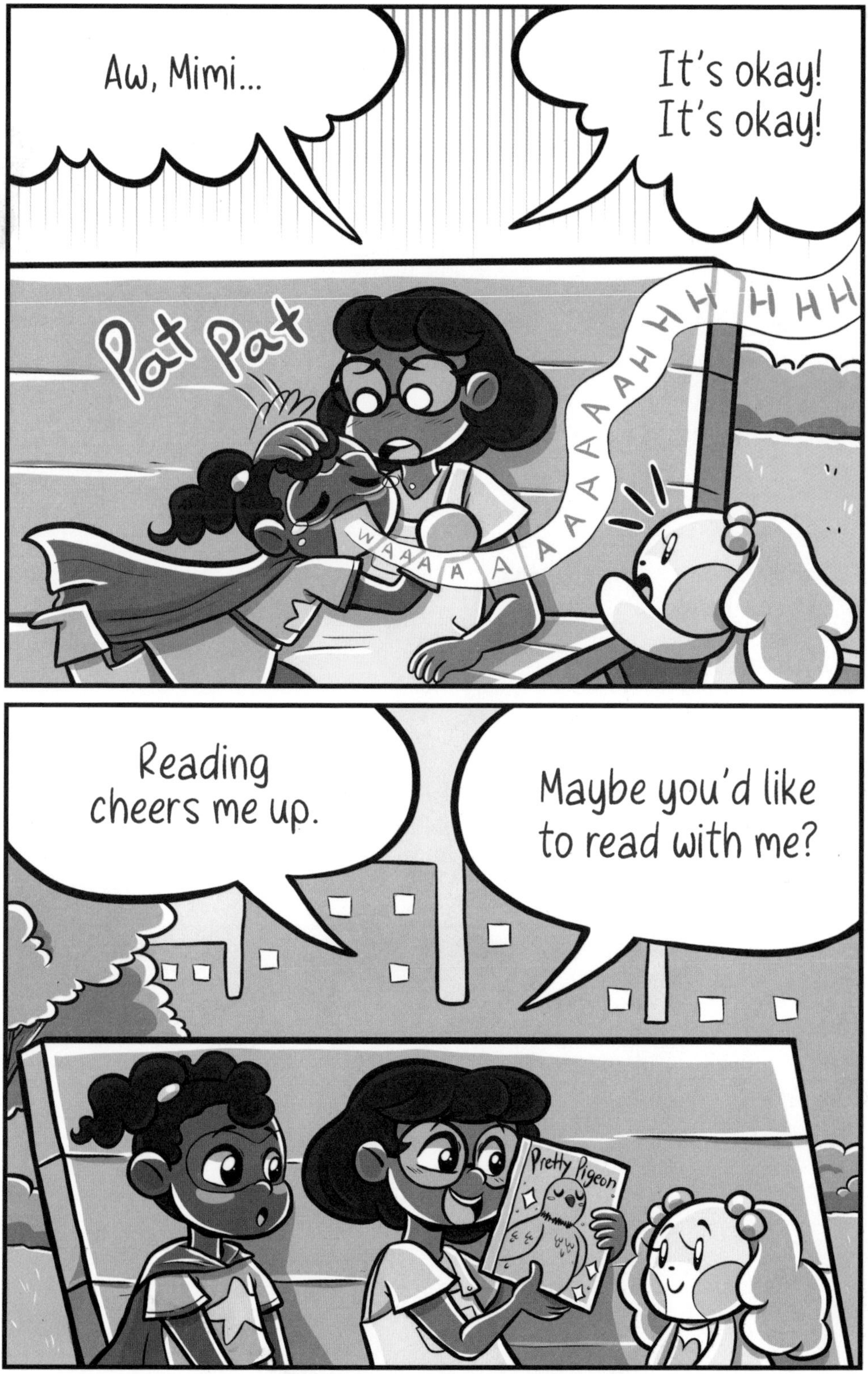
Aw, Mimi...
It's okay!
It's okay!
Pat Pat
WAAAAAAAAAAAAAHHHHHHH
Reading cheers me up.
Maybe you'd like to read with me?
Pretty Pigeon

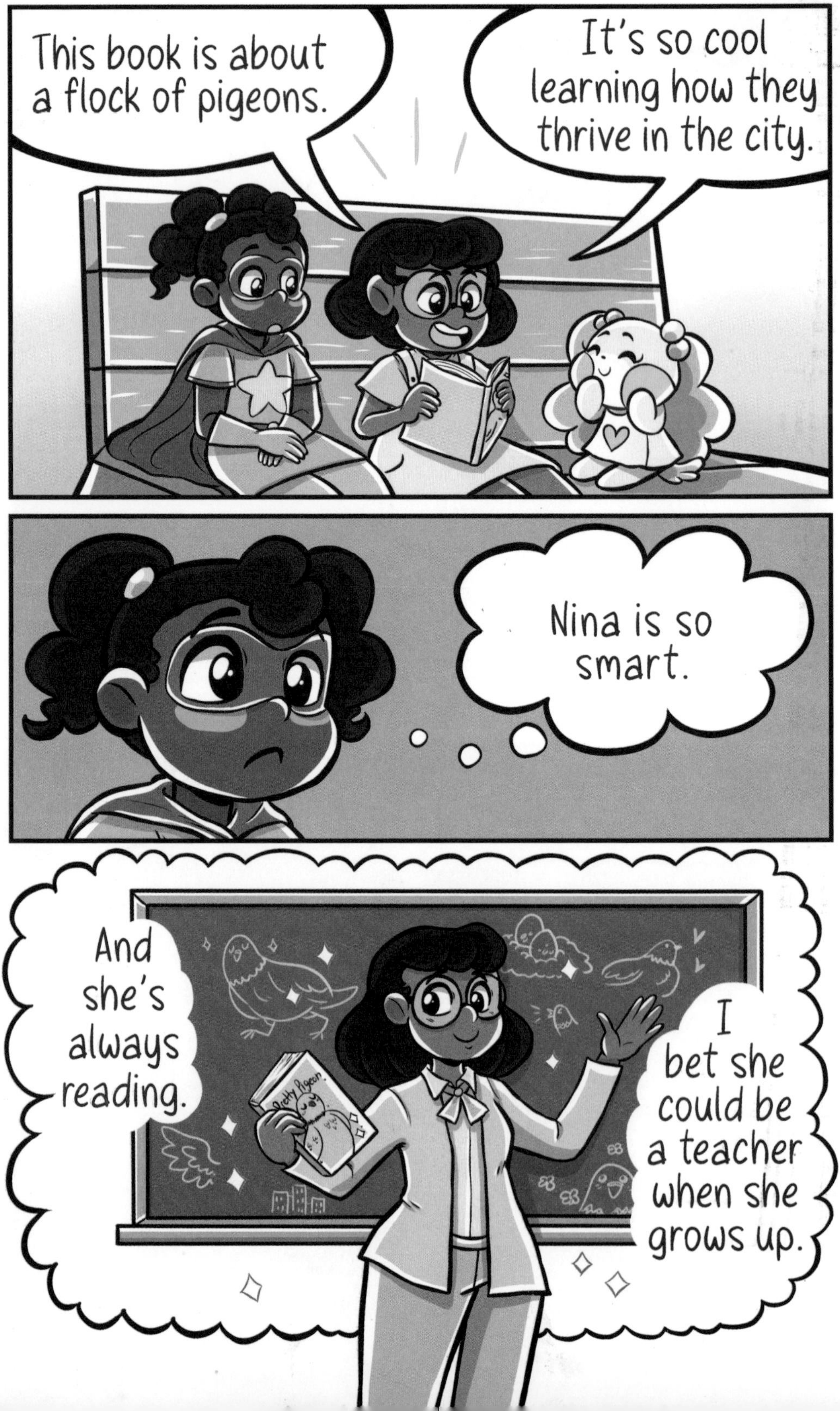

This book is about a flock of pigeons.
It's so cool learning how they thrive in the city.
Nina is so smart.
And she's always reading.
I bet she could be a teacher when she grows up.
Pretty Pigeon

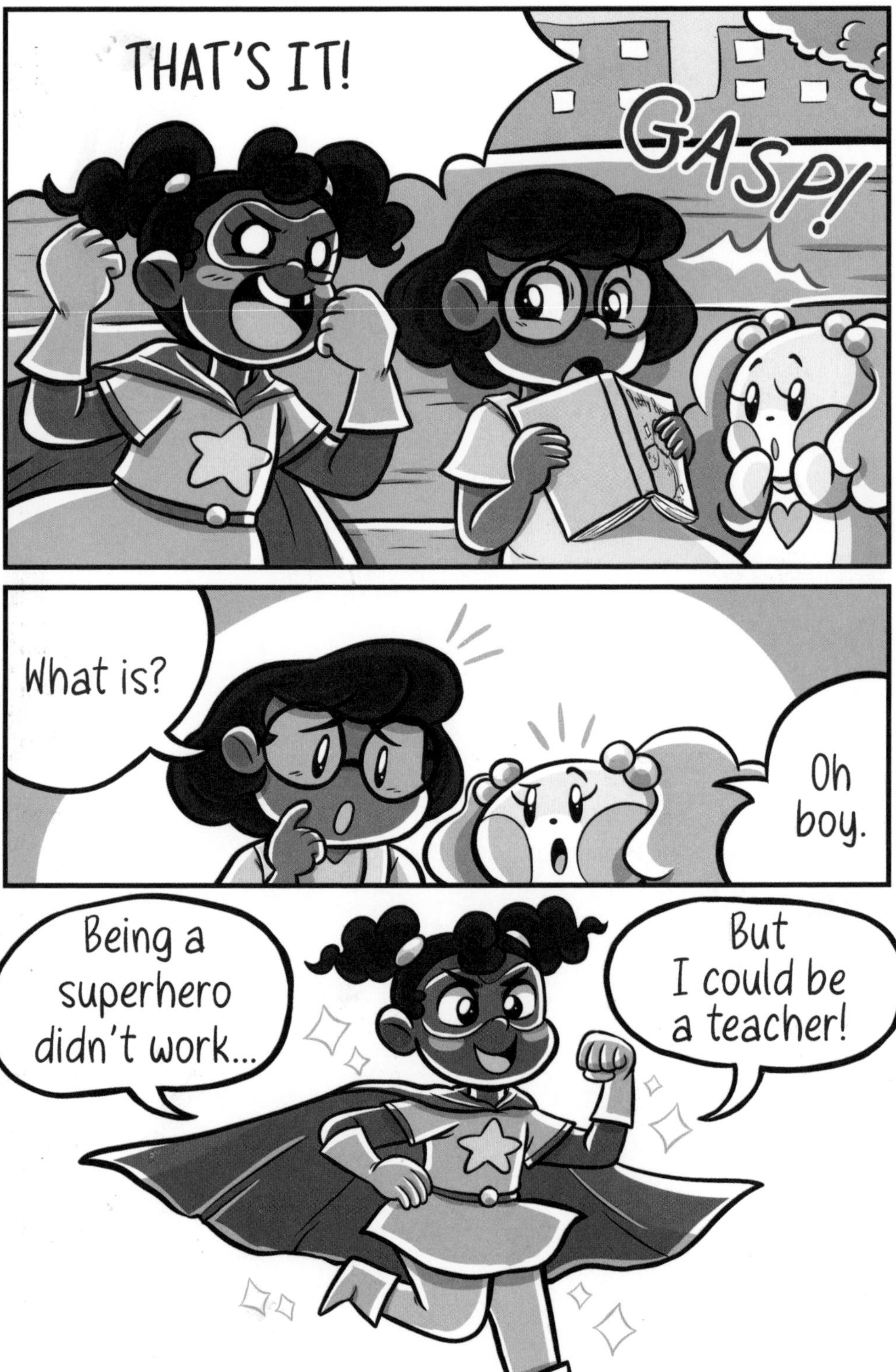
THAT'S IT!
GASP!
What is?
Oh boy.
Being a superhero didn't work...
But I could be a teacher!

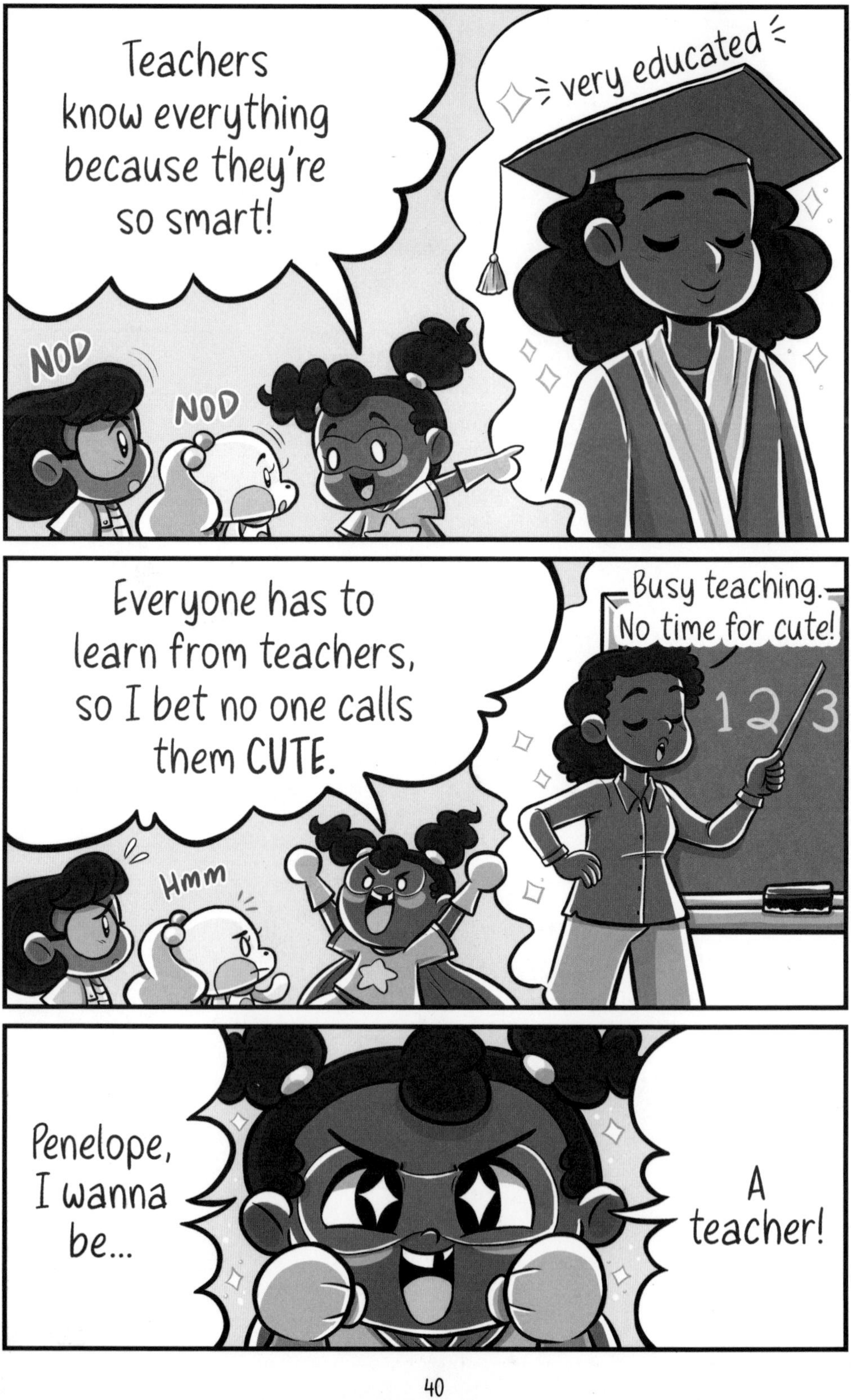
Teachers know everything because they're so smart!
very educated
NOD
NOD
Everyone has to learn from teachers, so I bet no one calls them CUTE.
Busy teaching. No time for cute!
1 2 3
Hmm
Penelope, I wanna be...
A teacher!

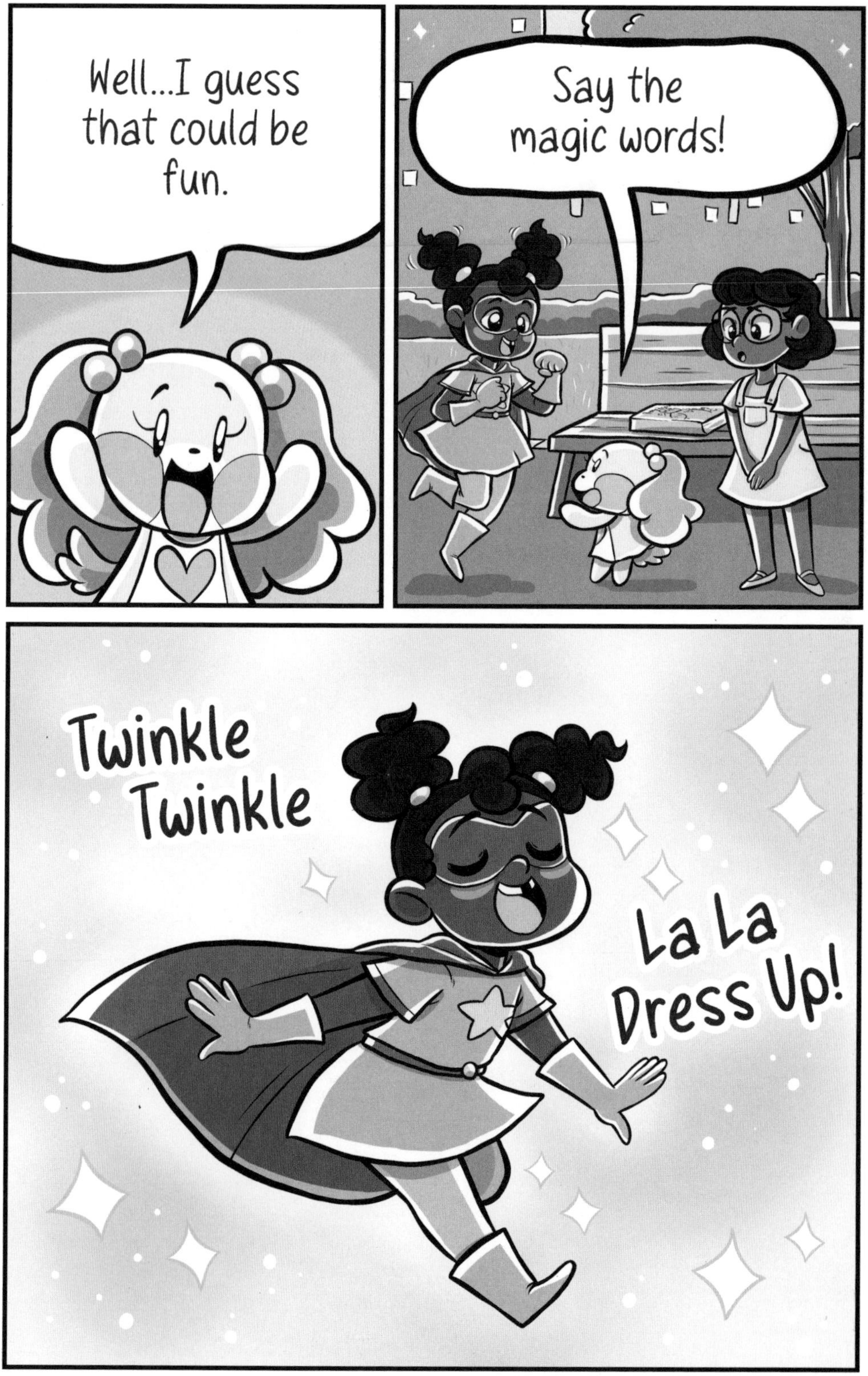
Well...I guess that could be fun.
Say the magic words!
Twinkle Twinkle
La La Dress Up!

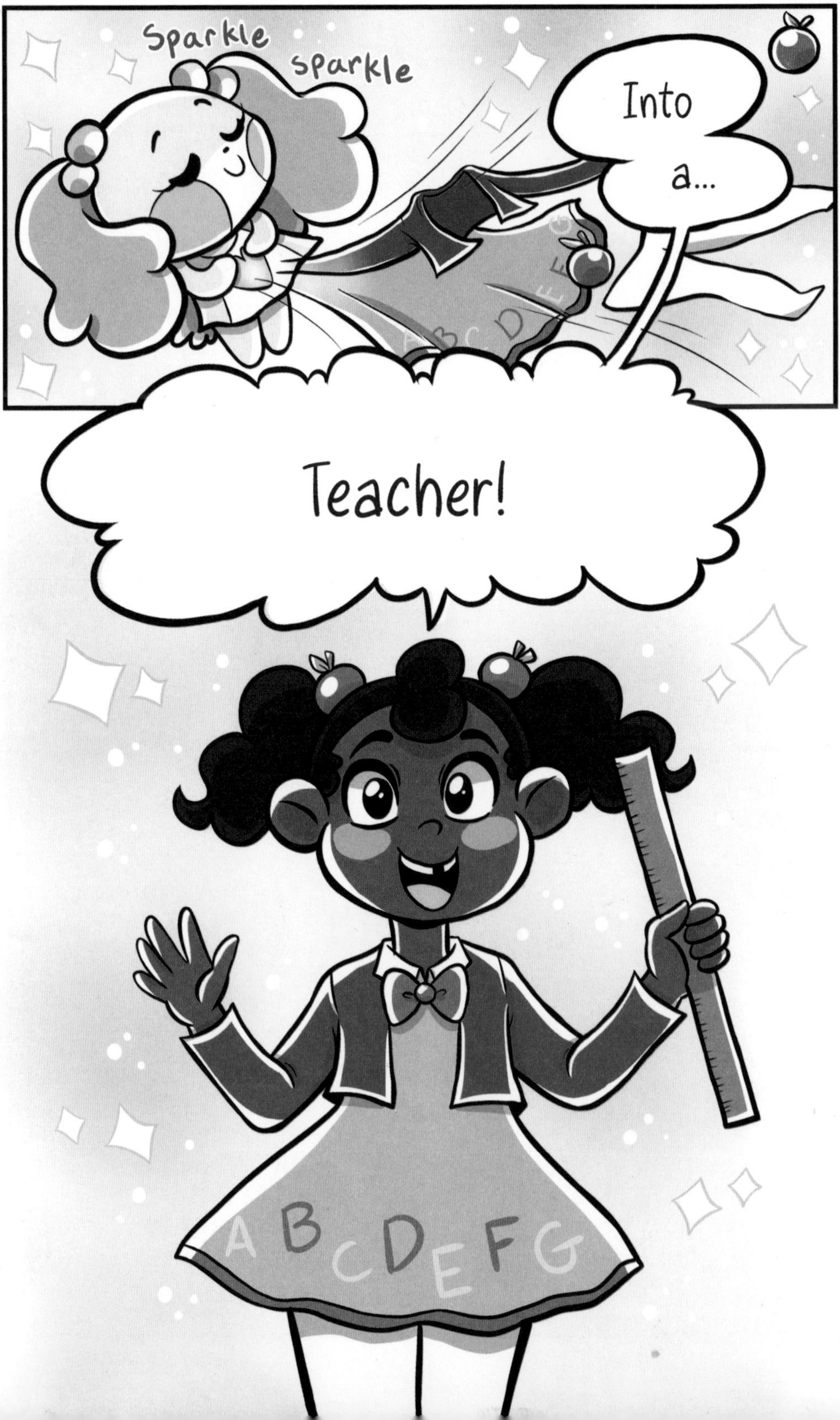
Sparkle
sparkle
Into a...
Teacher!
ABCDEFG

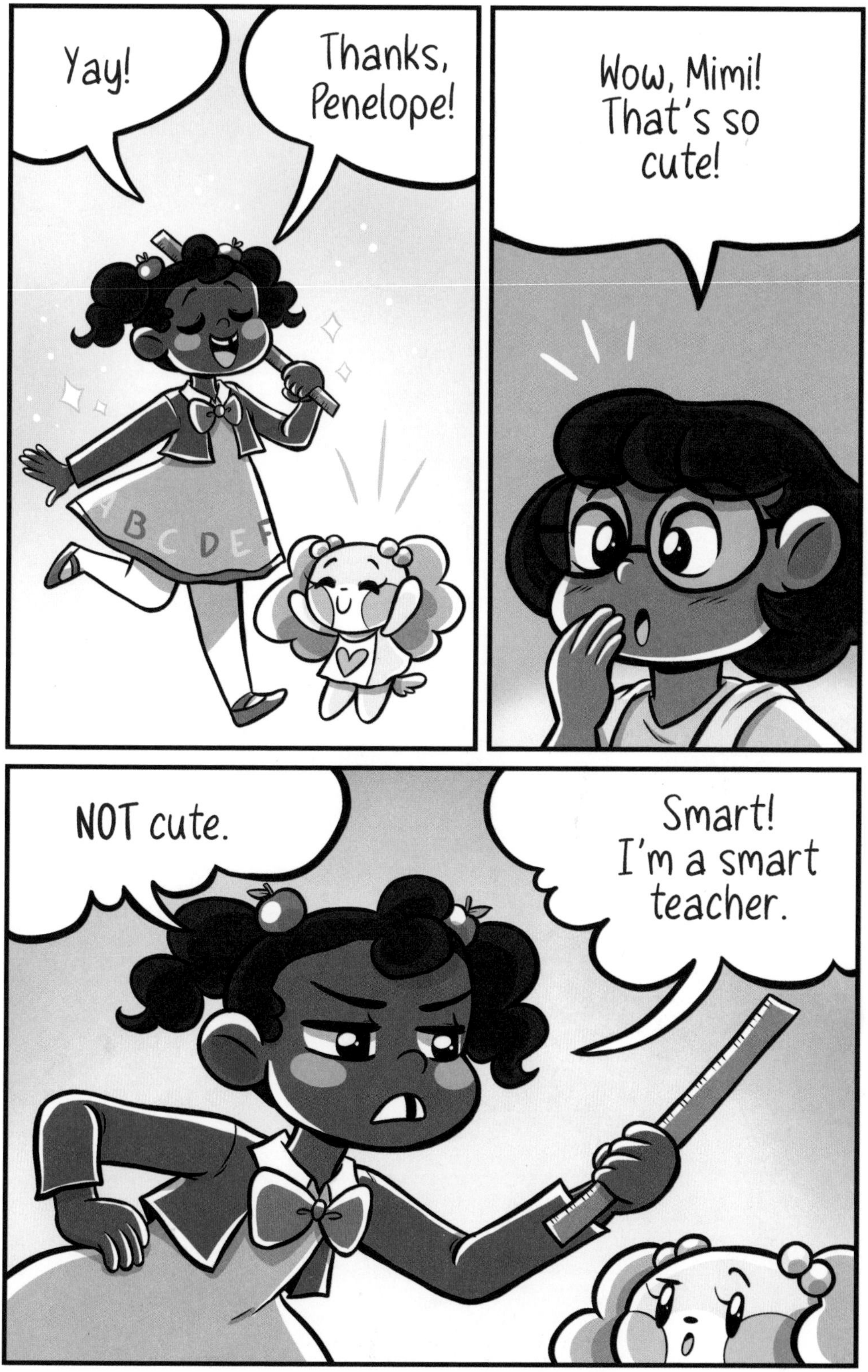
Yay!
Thanks, Penelope!
A B C D E F
Wow, Mimi! That's so cute!
NOT cute.
Smart! I'm a smart teacher.

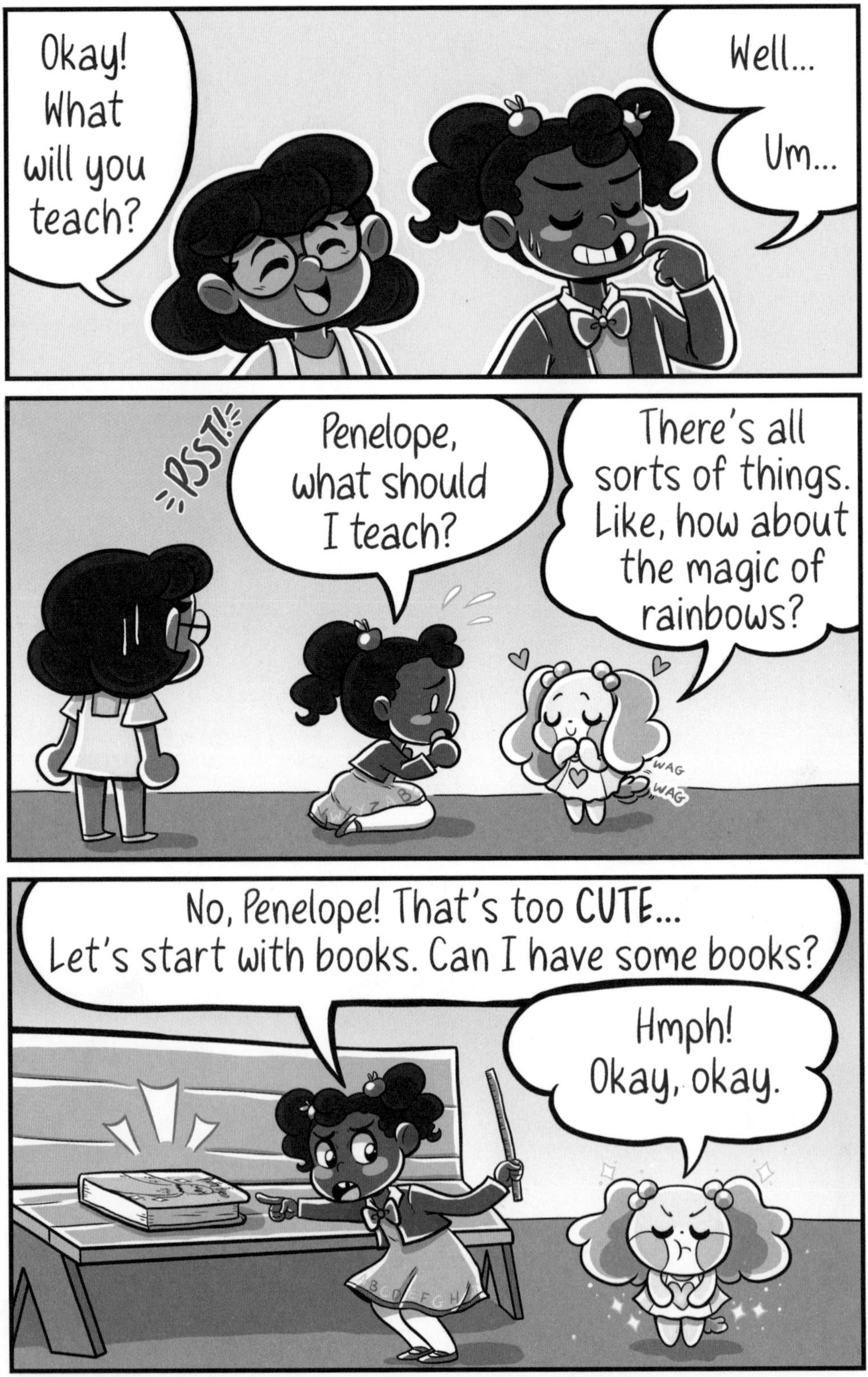
Okay! What will you teach?
Well...
Um...
PSST!
Penelope, what should I teach?
There's all sorts of things. Like, how about the magic of rainbows?
WAG
WAG
No, Penelope! That's too CUTE...
Let's start with books. Can I have some books?
Hmph! Okay, okay.

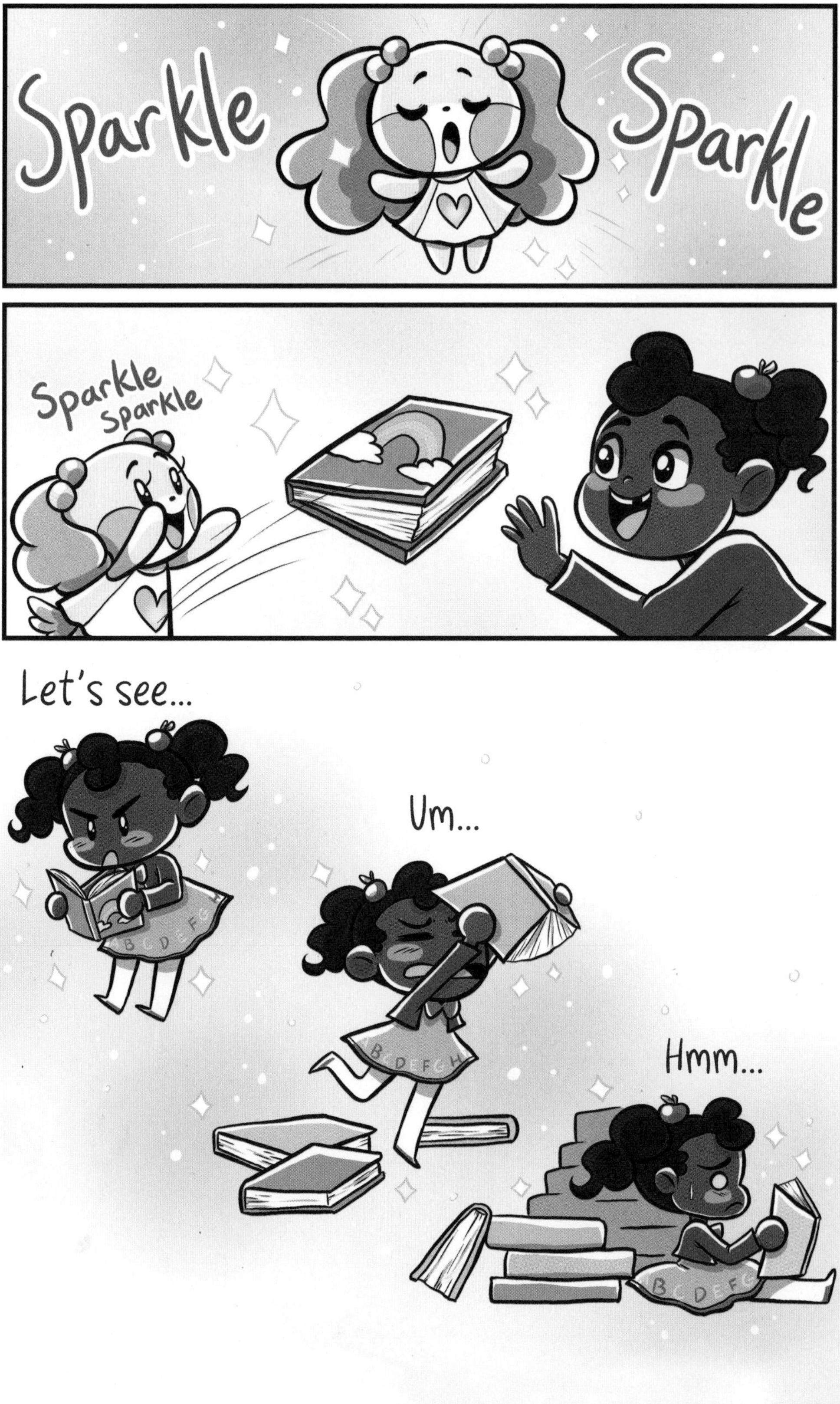
Sparkle
Sparkle
Sparkle
sparkle
Let's see...
Um...
Hmm...

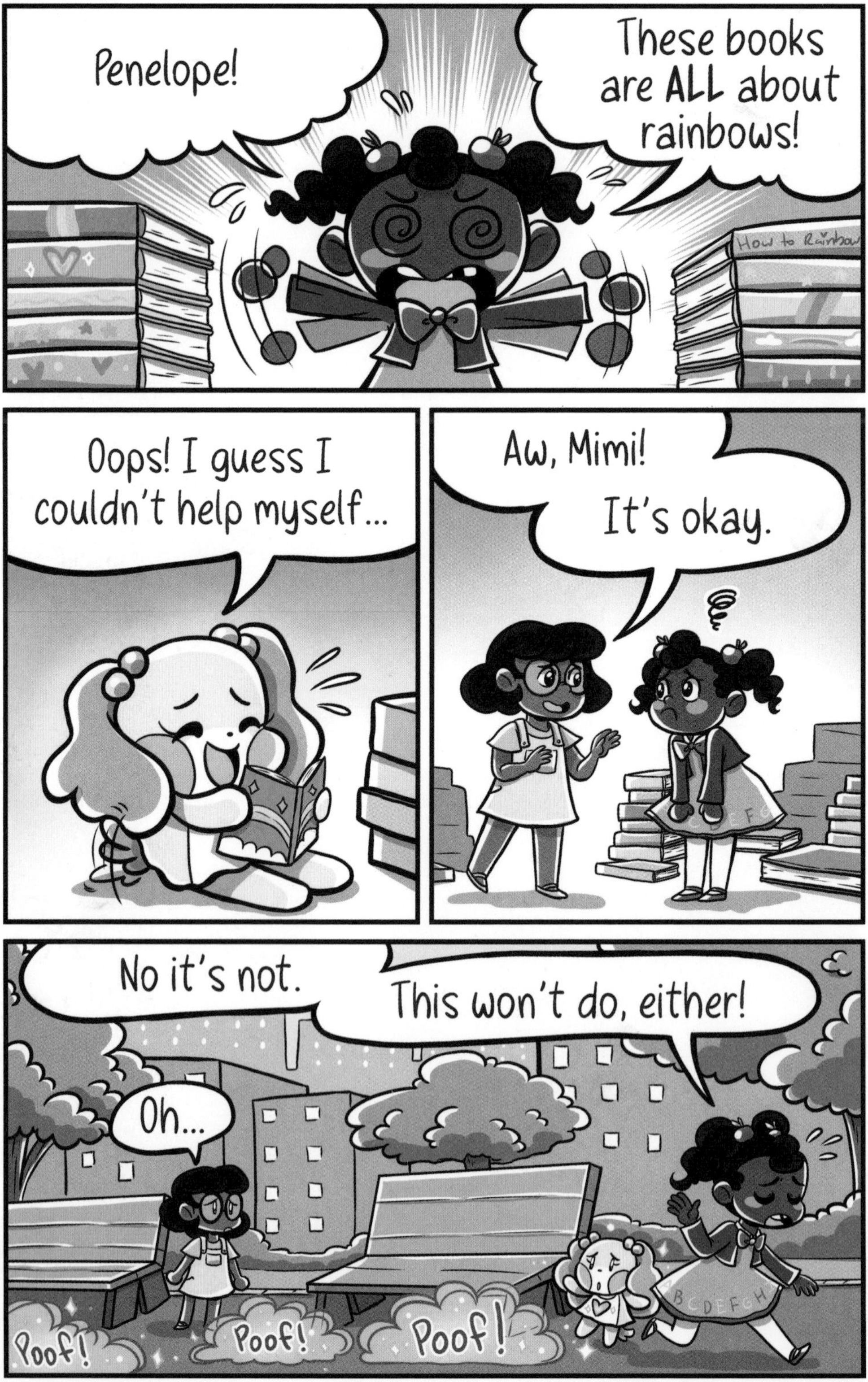
Penelope!
These books are ALL about rainbows!
How to Rainbow
Oops! I guess I couldn't help myself...
Aw, Mimi!
It's okay.
No it's not.
This won't do, either!
Oh...
Poof!
Poof!
Poof!

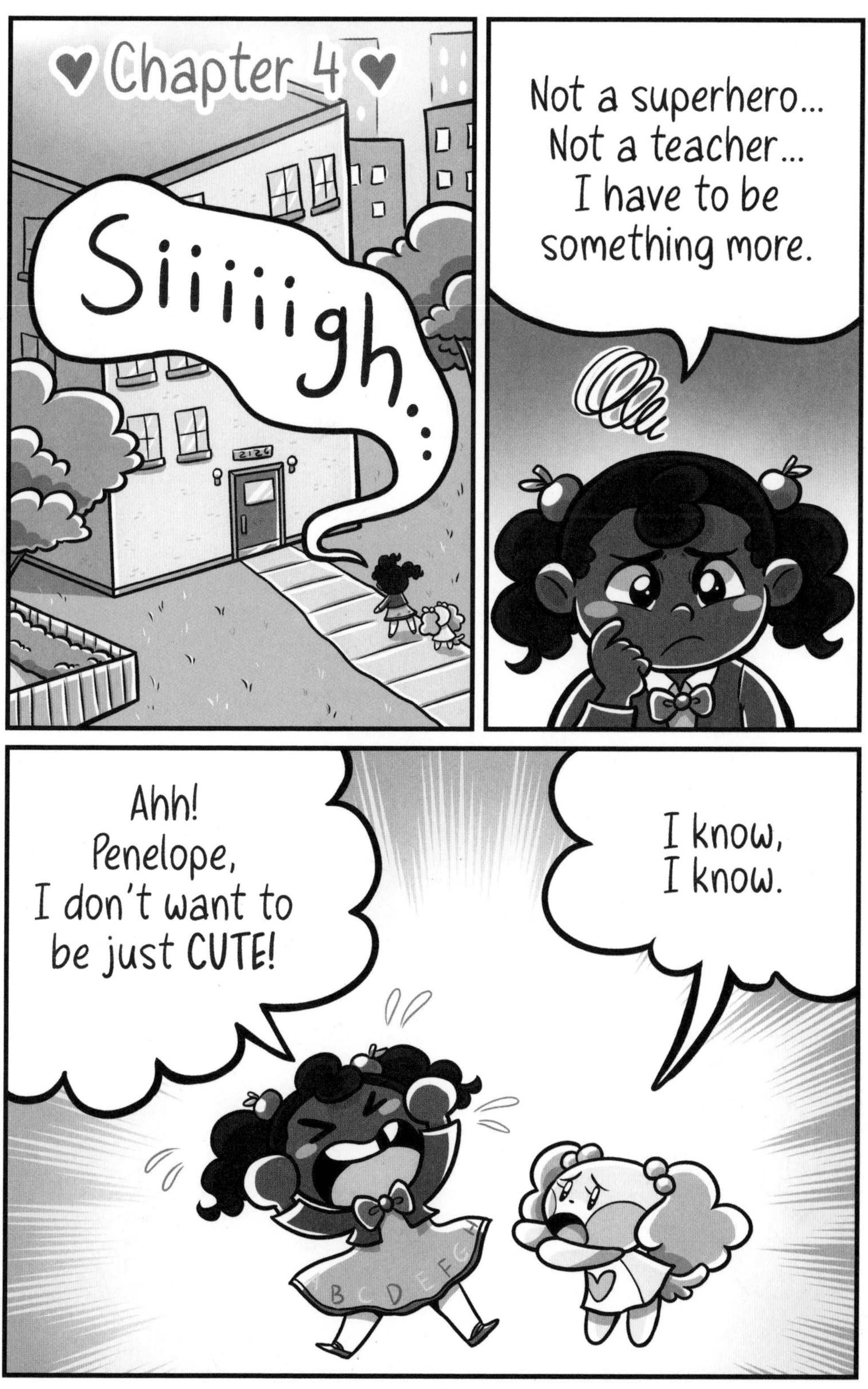
Chapter 4
Siiiiigh...
Not a superhero... Not a teacher... I have to be something more.
2126
Ahh! Penelope, I don't want to be just CUTE!
I know, I know.
A B C D E F G H

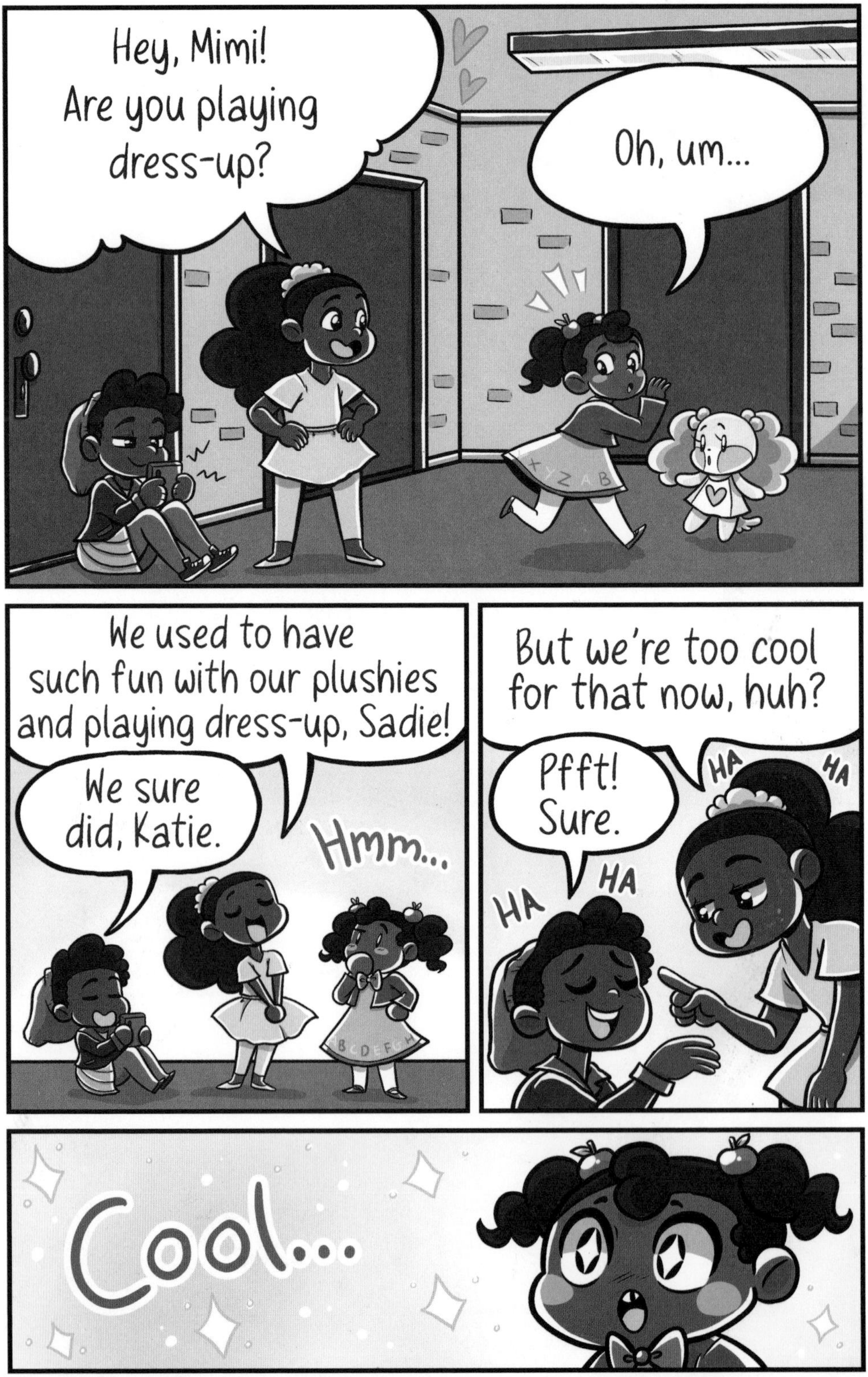
Hey, Mimi! Are you playing dress-up?
Oh, um...
We used to have such fun with our plushies and playing dress-up, Sadie!
We sure did, Katie.
Hmm...
But we're too cool for that now, huh?
Pfft! Sure.
HA HA
HA HA
Cool...

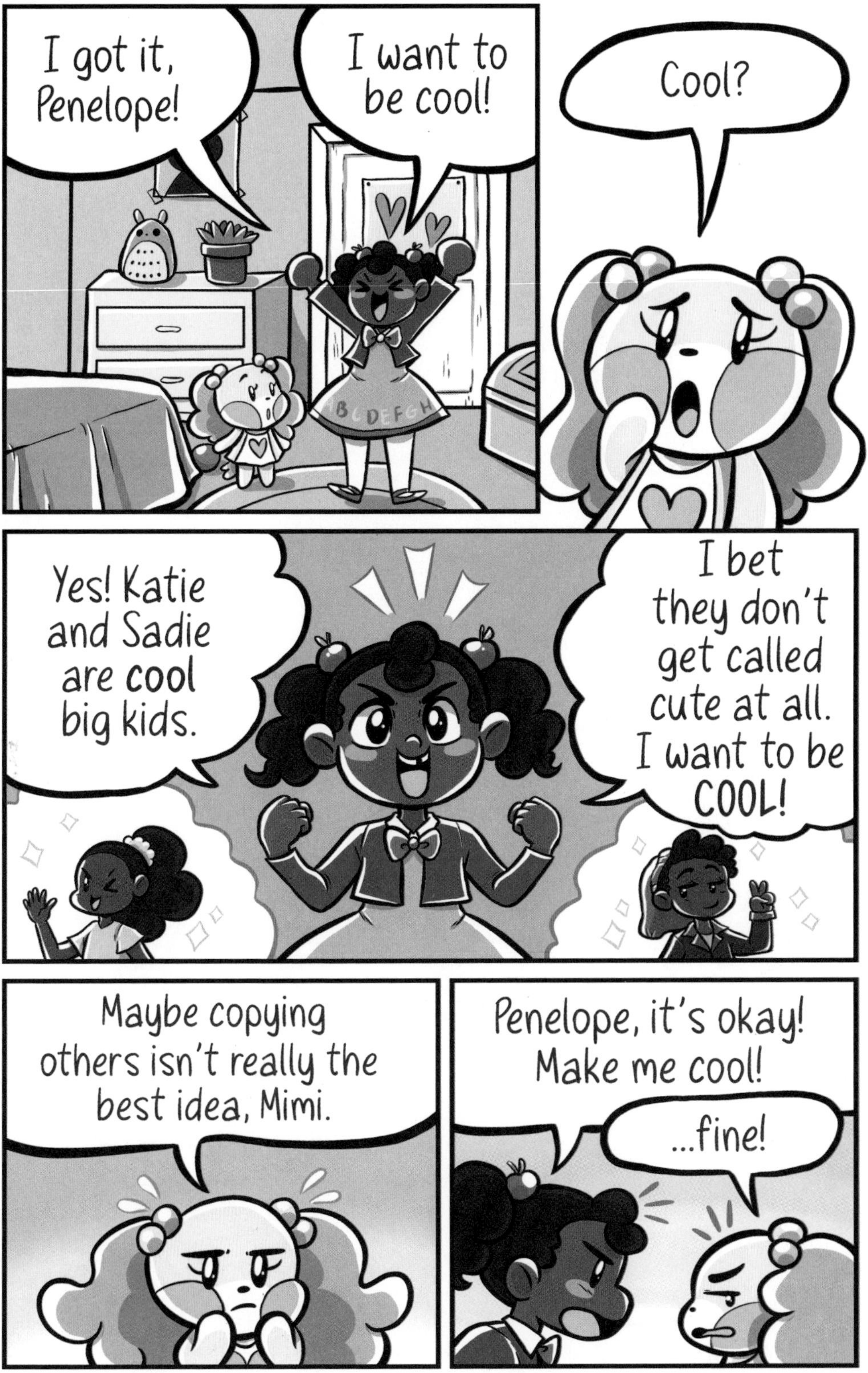
I got it, Penelope!
I want to be cool!
Cool?
Yes! Katie and Sadie are **cool** big kids.
I bet they don't get called cute at all. I want to be **COOL**!
Maybe copying others isn't really the best idea, Mimi.
Penelope, it's okay! Make me cool!
...fine!

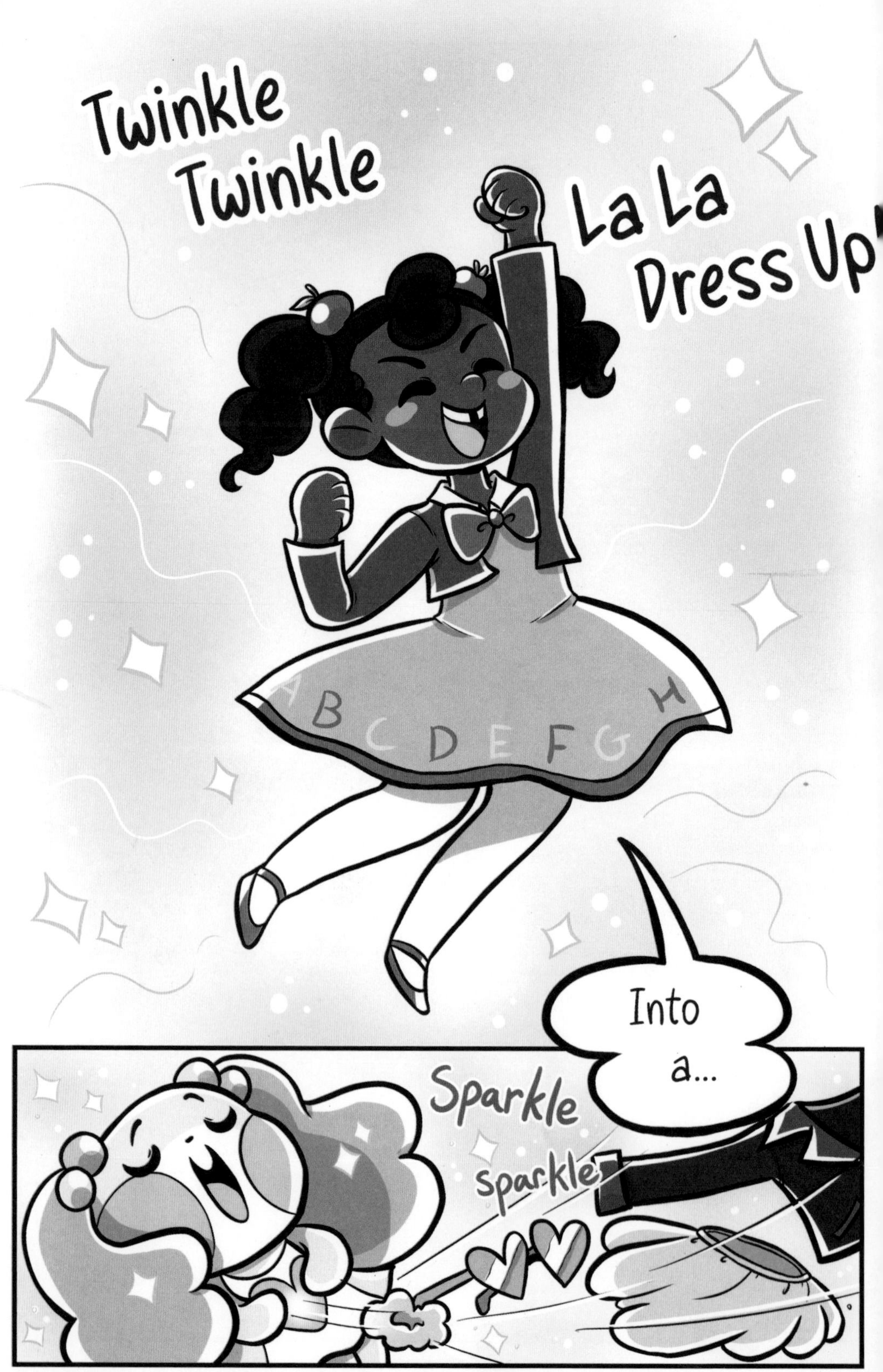
Twinkle
Twinkle
La La
Dress Up!
A B C D E F G H
Into a...
Sparkle
sparkle

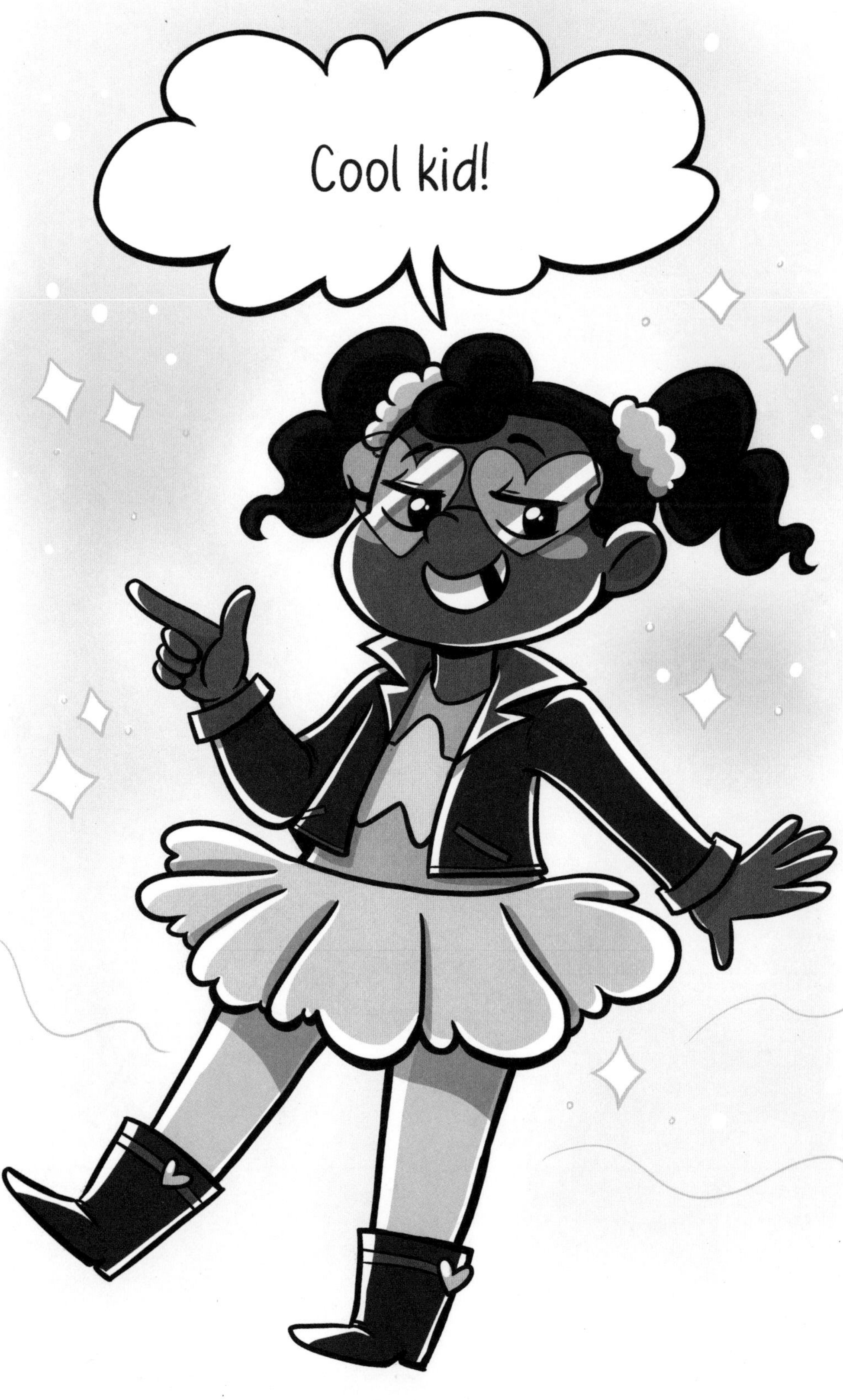
Cool kid!

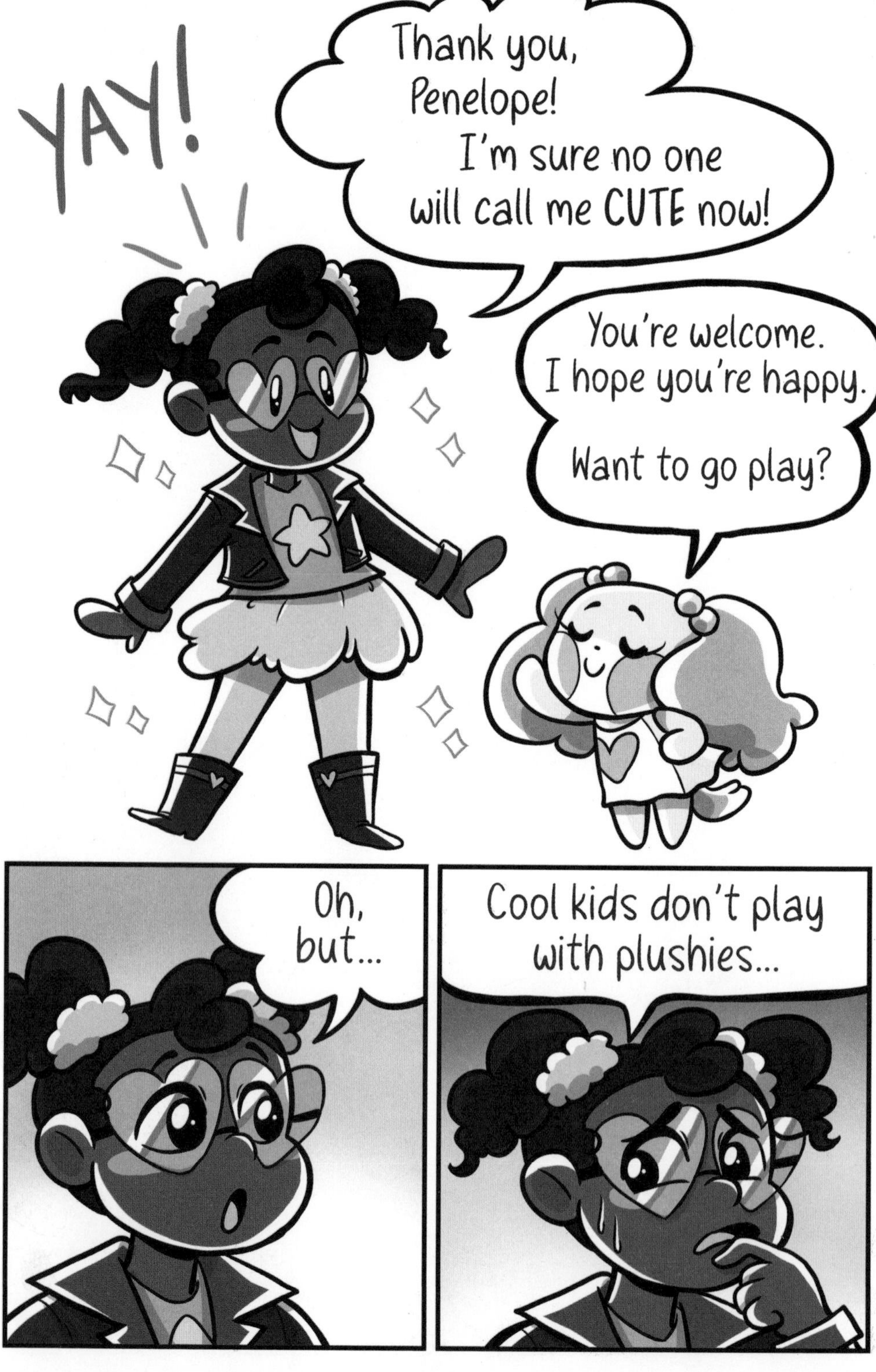
YAY!
Thank you, Penelope! I'm sure no one will call me CUTE now!
You're welcome. I hope you're happy.
Want to go play?
Oh, but...
Cool kids don't play with plushies...

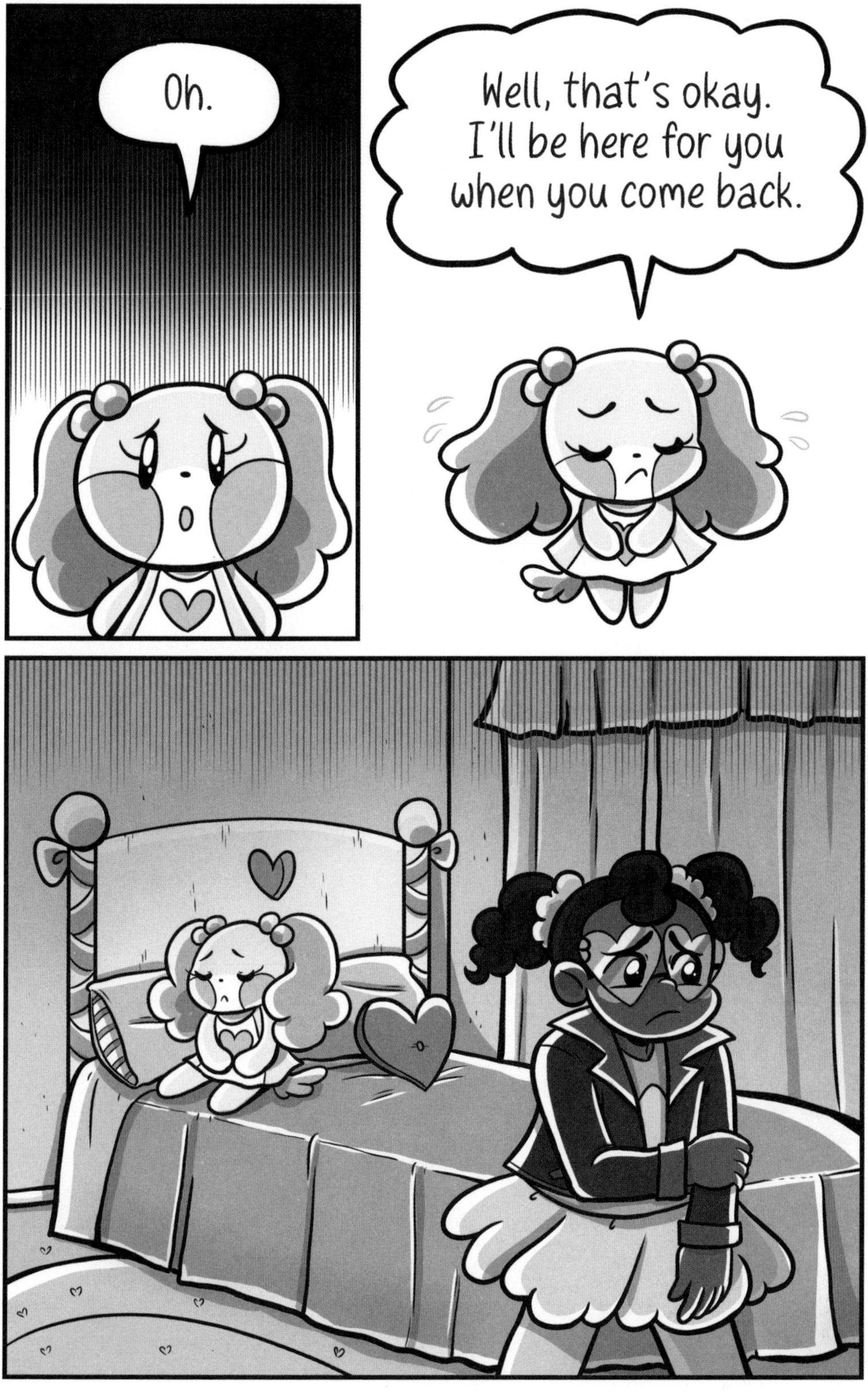
Oh.
Well, that's okay. I'll be here for you when you come back.

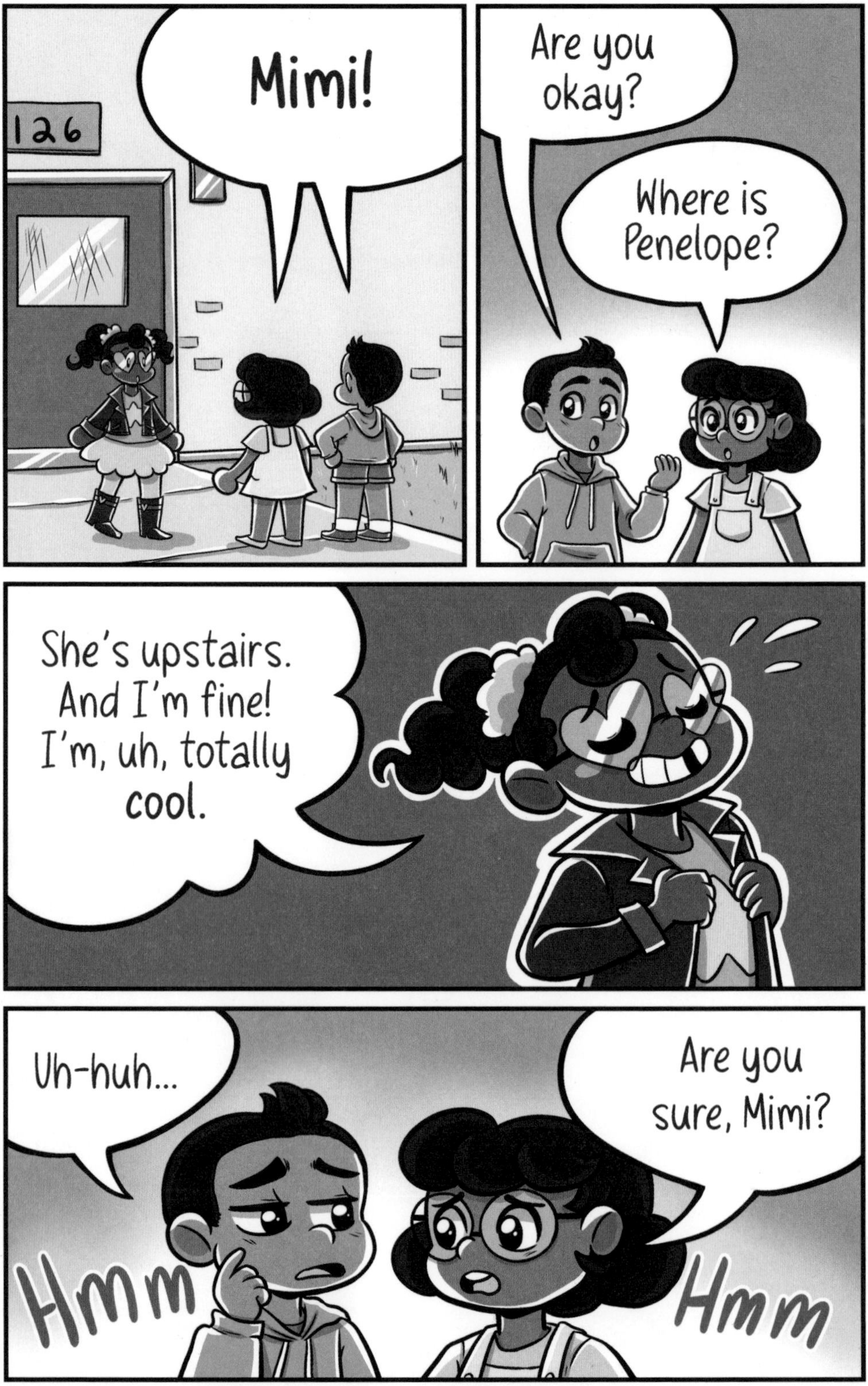
Mimi!
126
Are you okay?
Where is Penelope?
She's upstairs. And I'm fine! I'm, uh, totally cool.
Uh-huh...
Are you sure, Mimi?
Hmm
Hmm

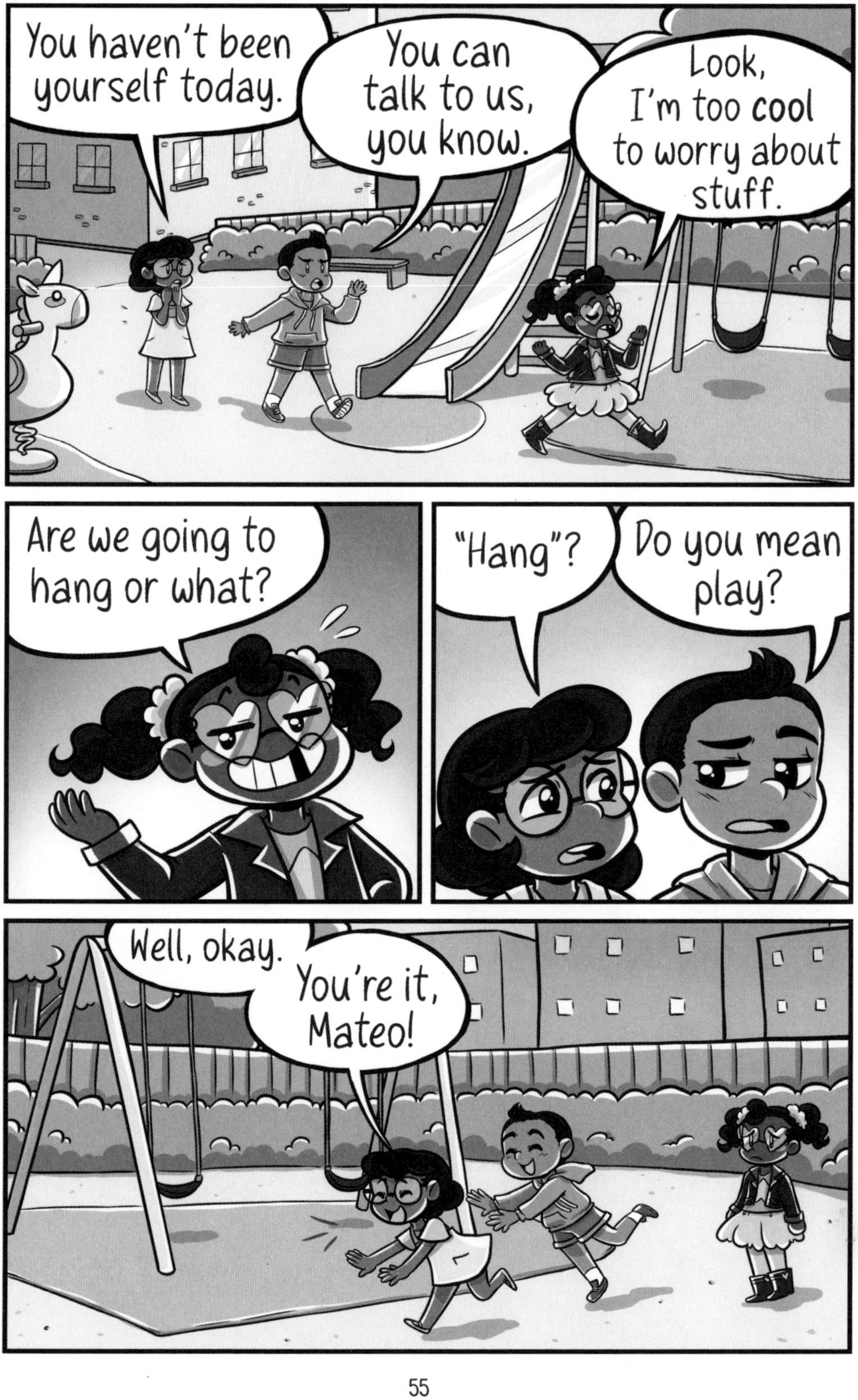
You haven't been yourself today.
You can talk to us, you know.
Look, I'm too cool to worry about stuff.
Are we going to hang or what?
"Hang"?
Do you mean play?
Well, okay.
You're it, Mateo!

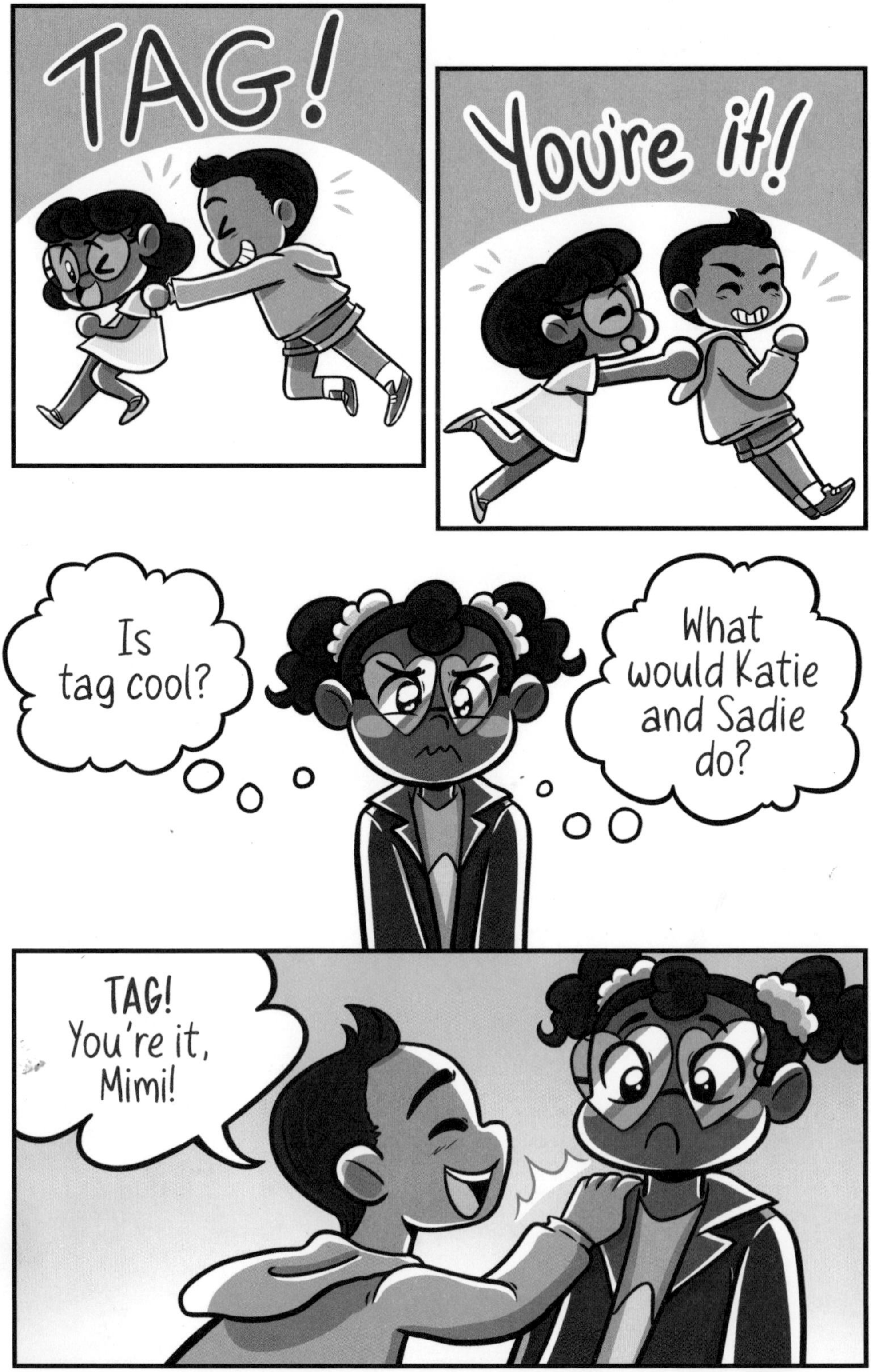
TAG!
You're it!
Is tag cool?
What would Katie and Sadie do?
TAG! You're it, Mimi!

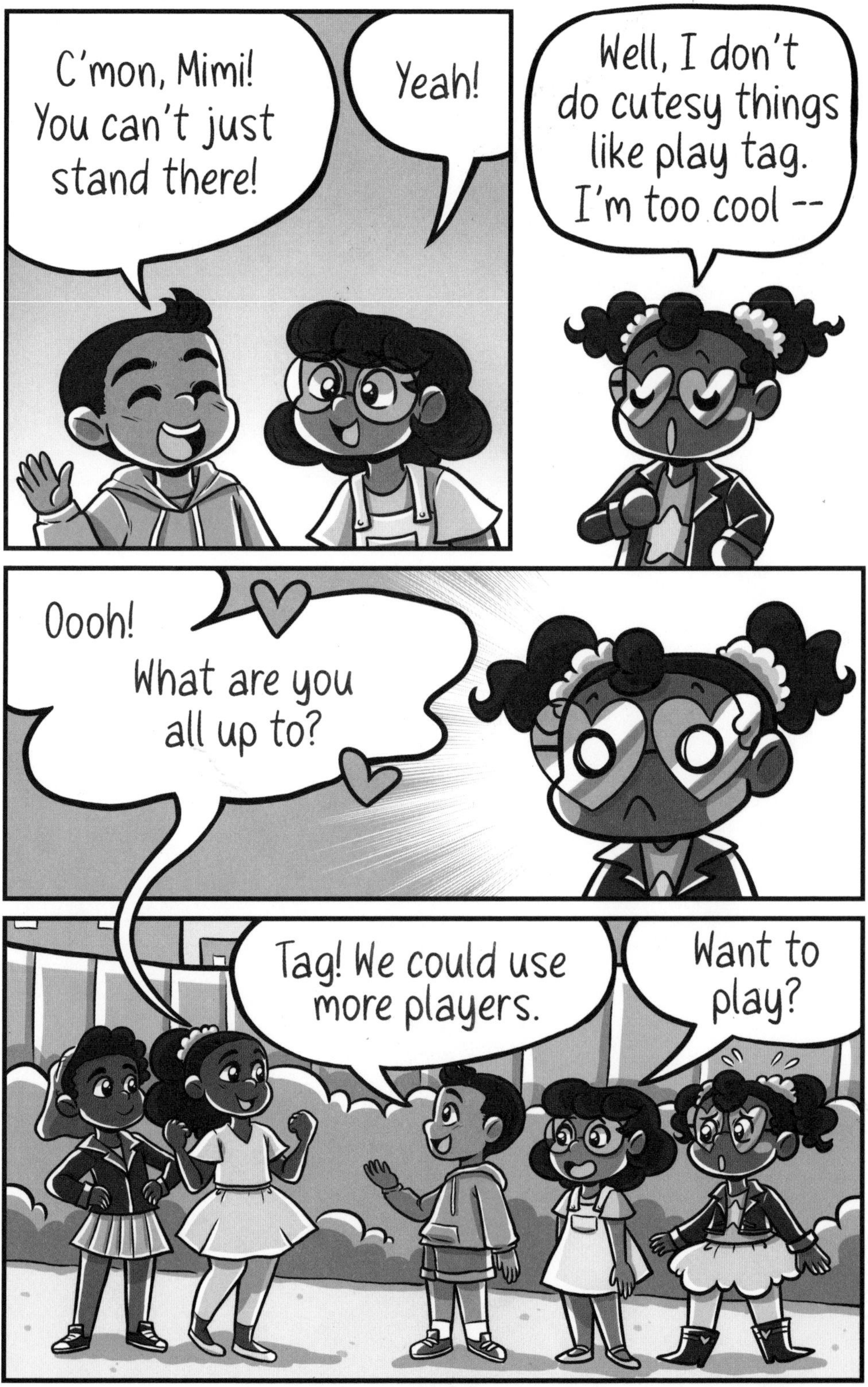
C'mon, Mimi! You can't just stand there!
Yeah!
Well, I don't do cutesy things like play tag. I'm too cool --
Oooh!
What are you all up to?
Tag! We could use more players.
Want to play?

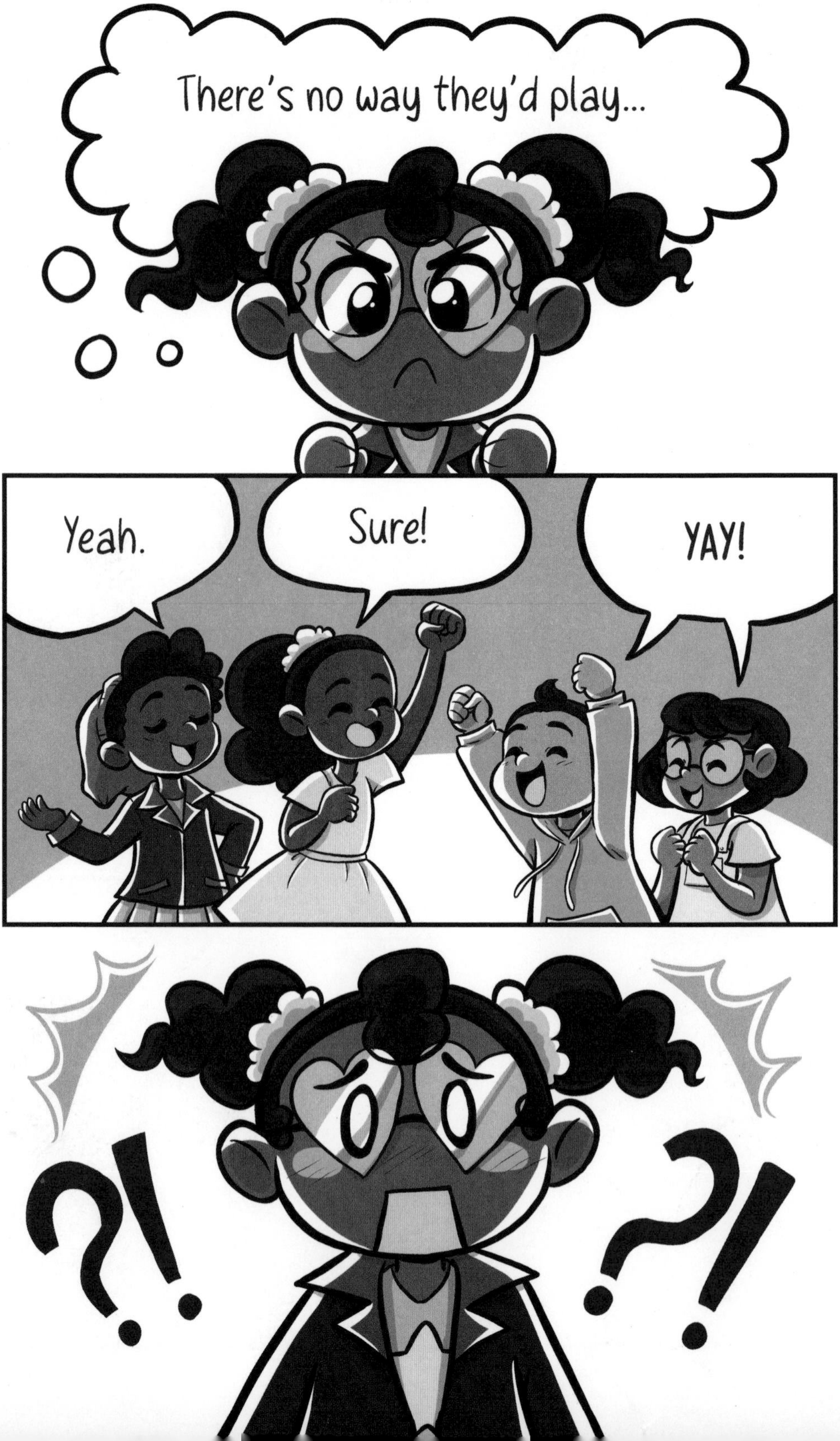
There's no way they'd play...
Yeah.
Sure!
YAY!
?!
?!

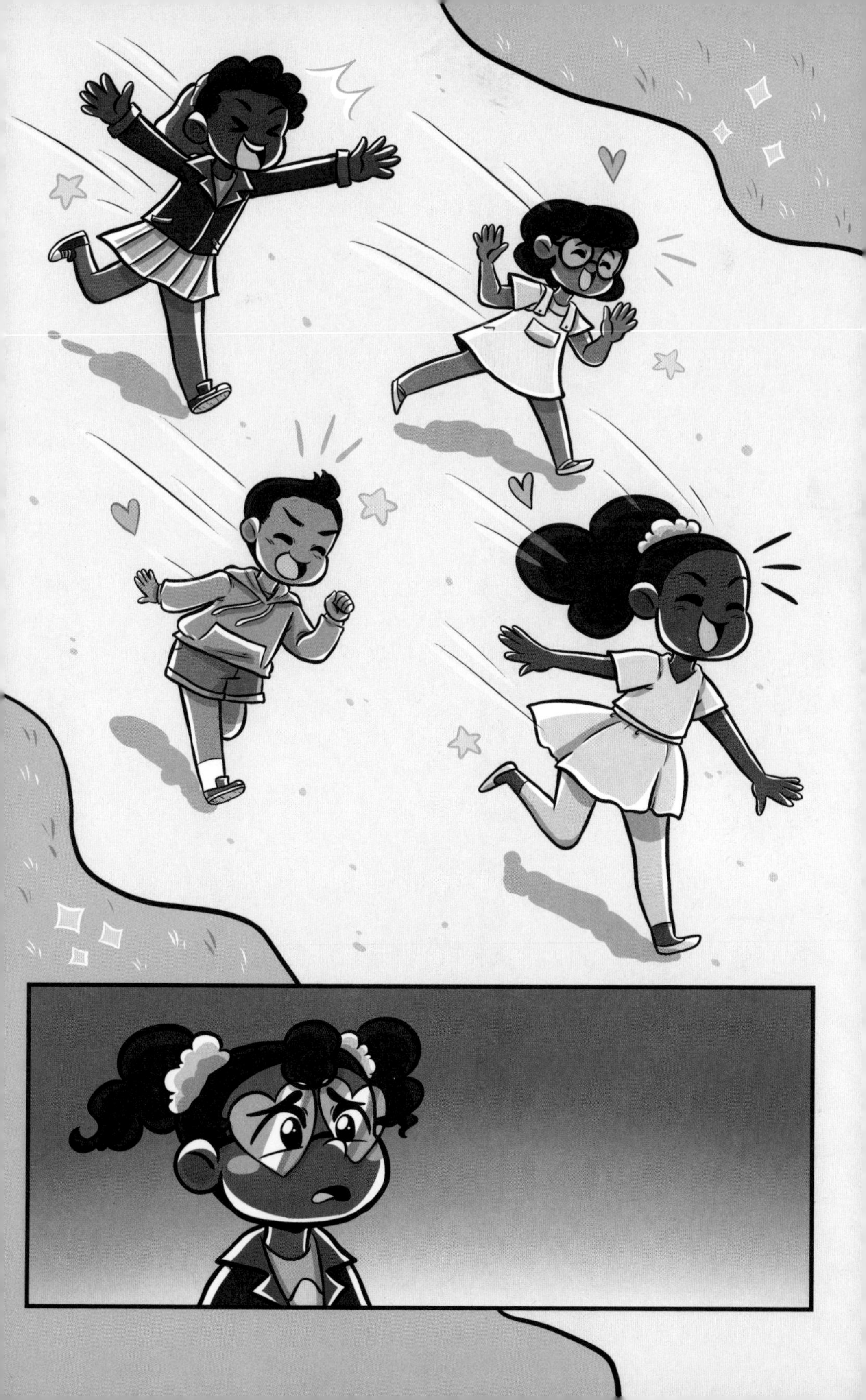

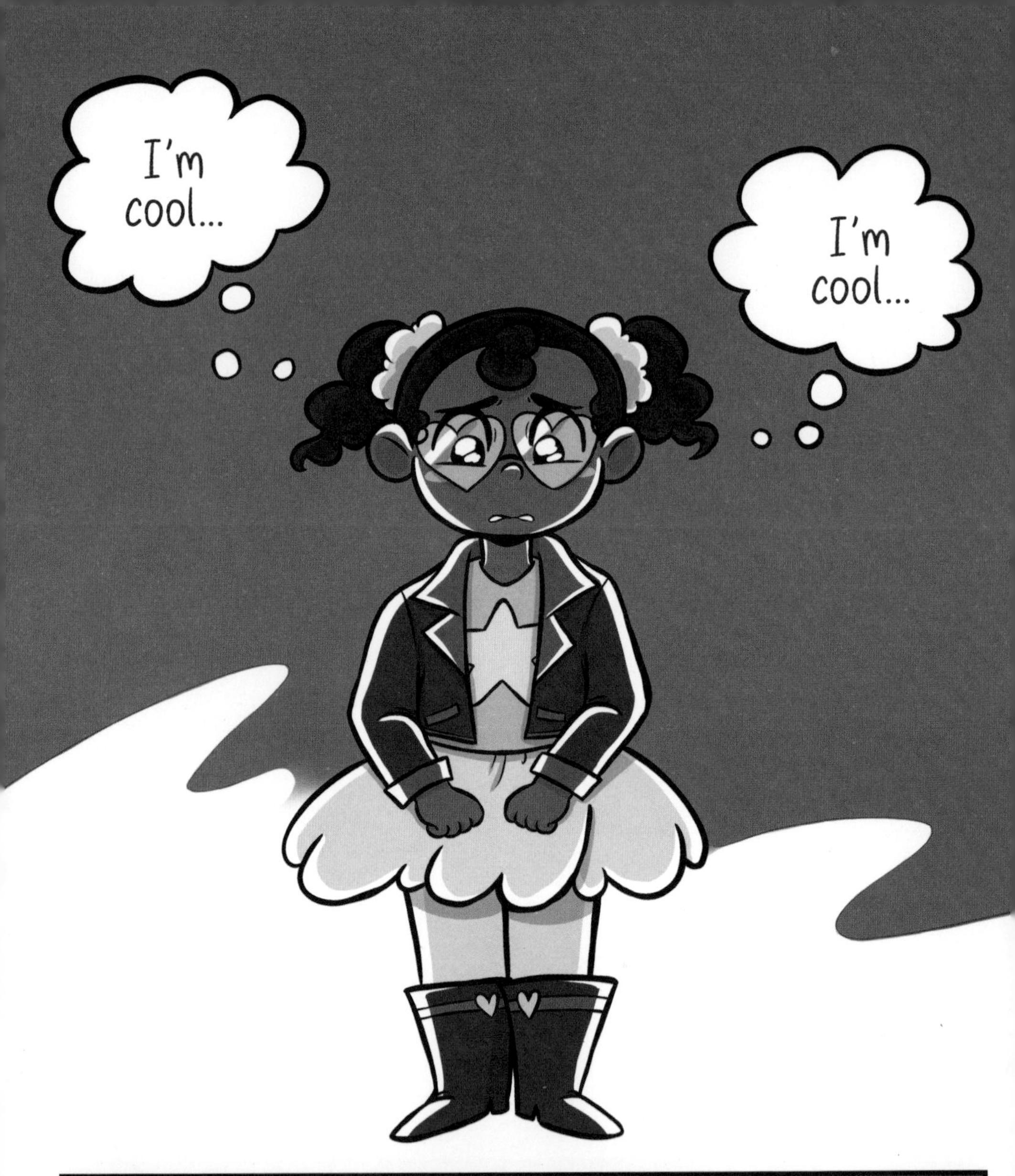
I'm cool...
I'm cool...

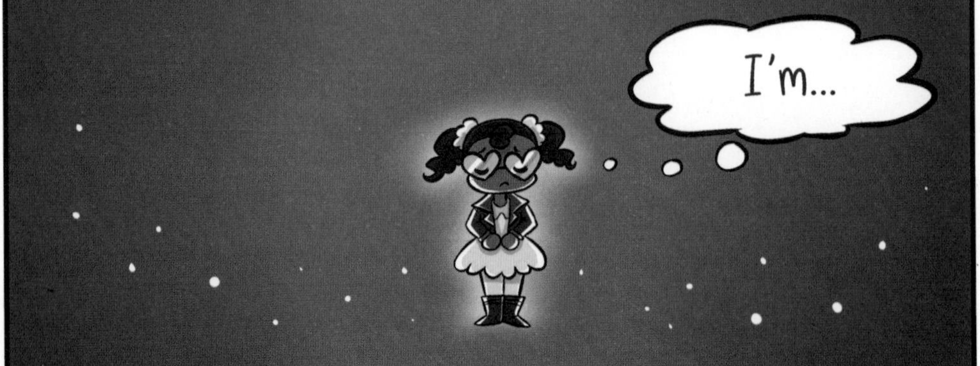
I'm...

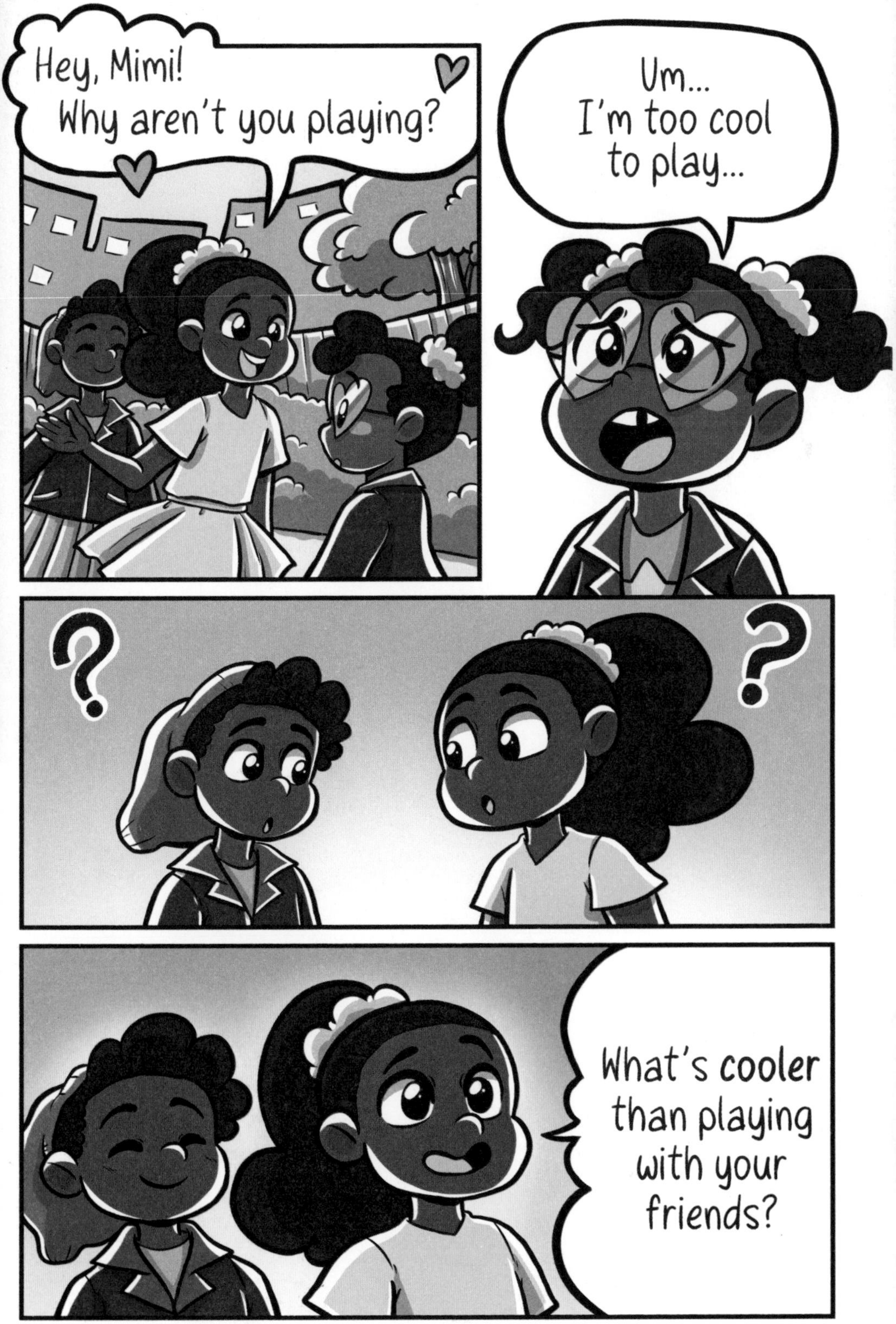
Hey, Mimi!
Why aren't you playing?
Um...
I'm too cool
to play...
What's cooler
than playing
with your
friends?

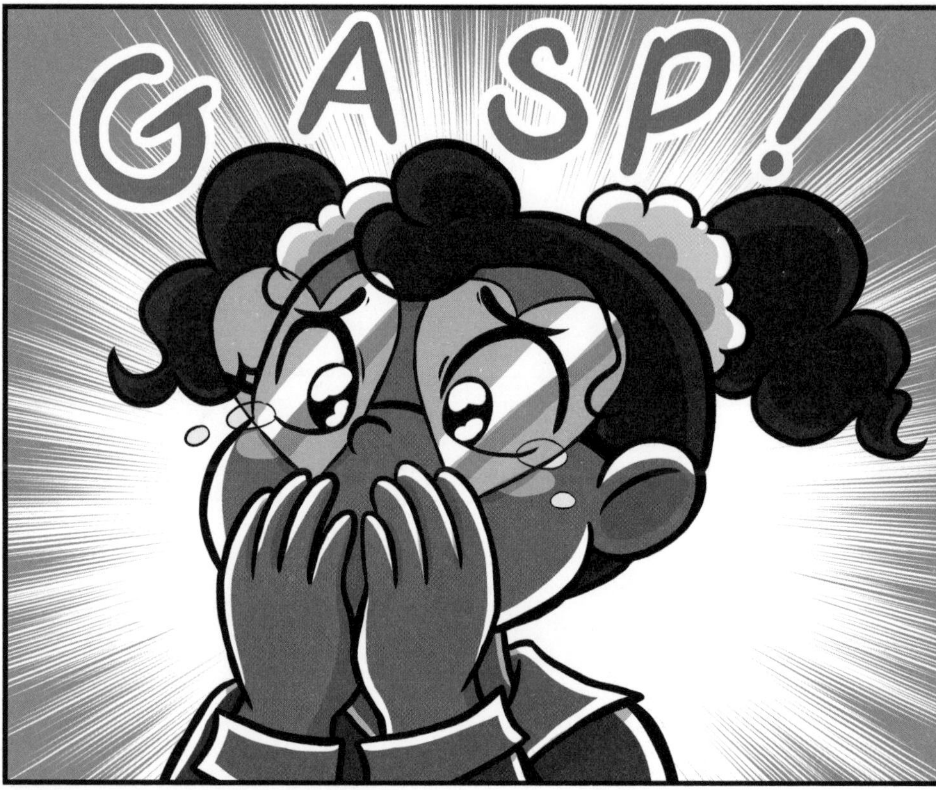
GASP!

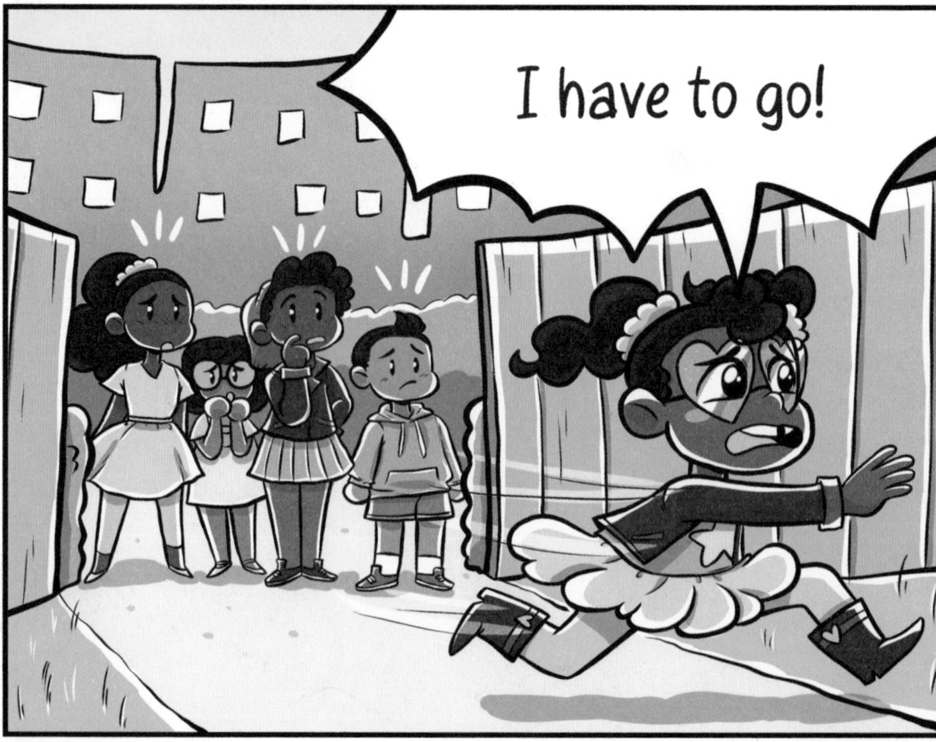
I have to go!

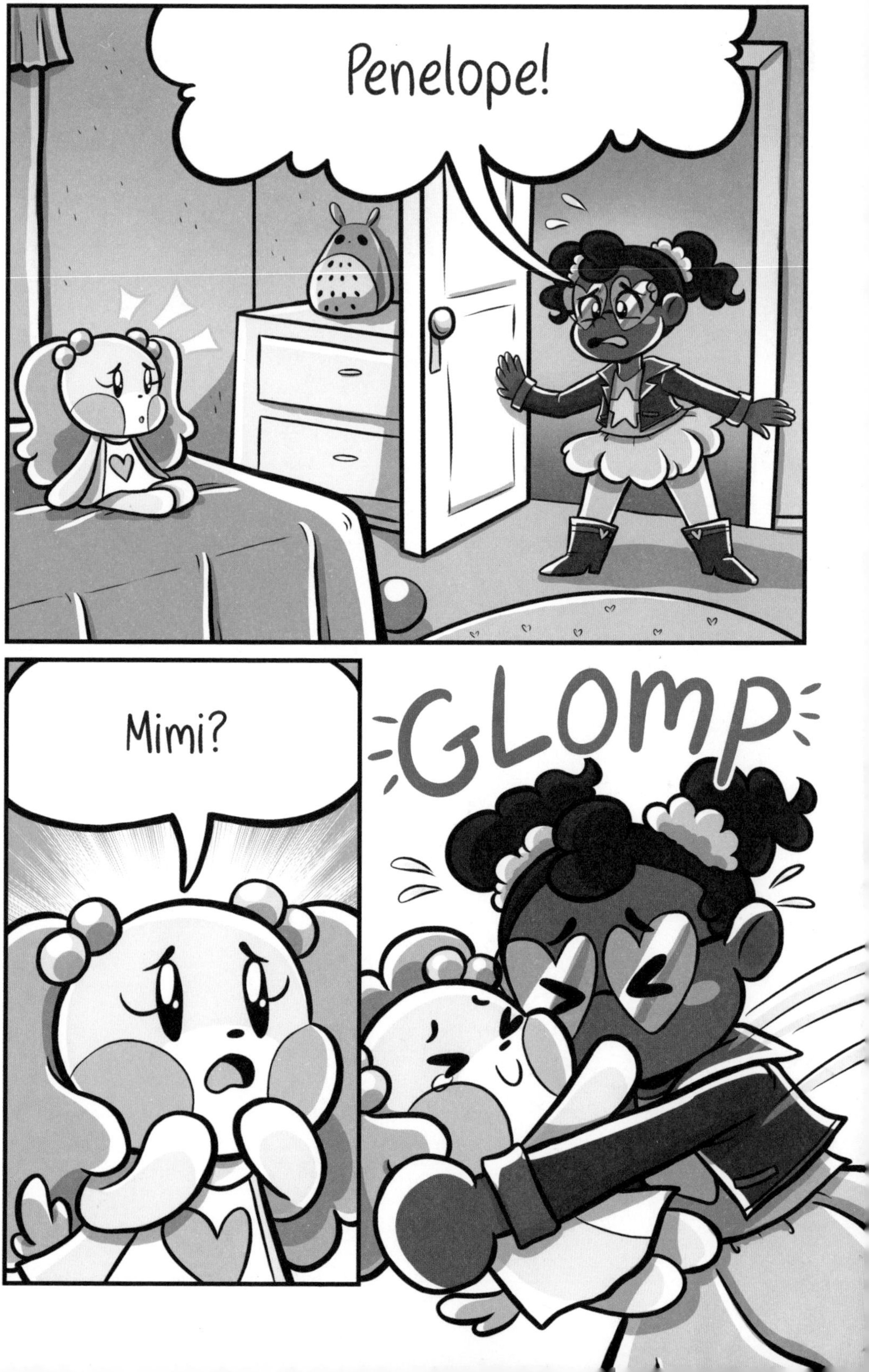
Penelope!
Mimi?
GLOMP

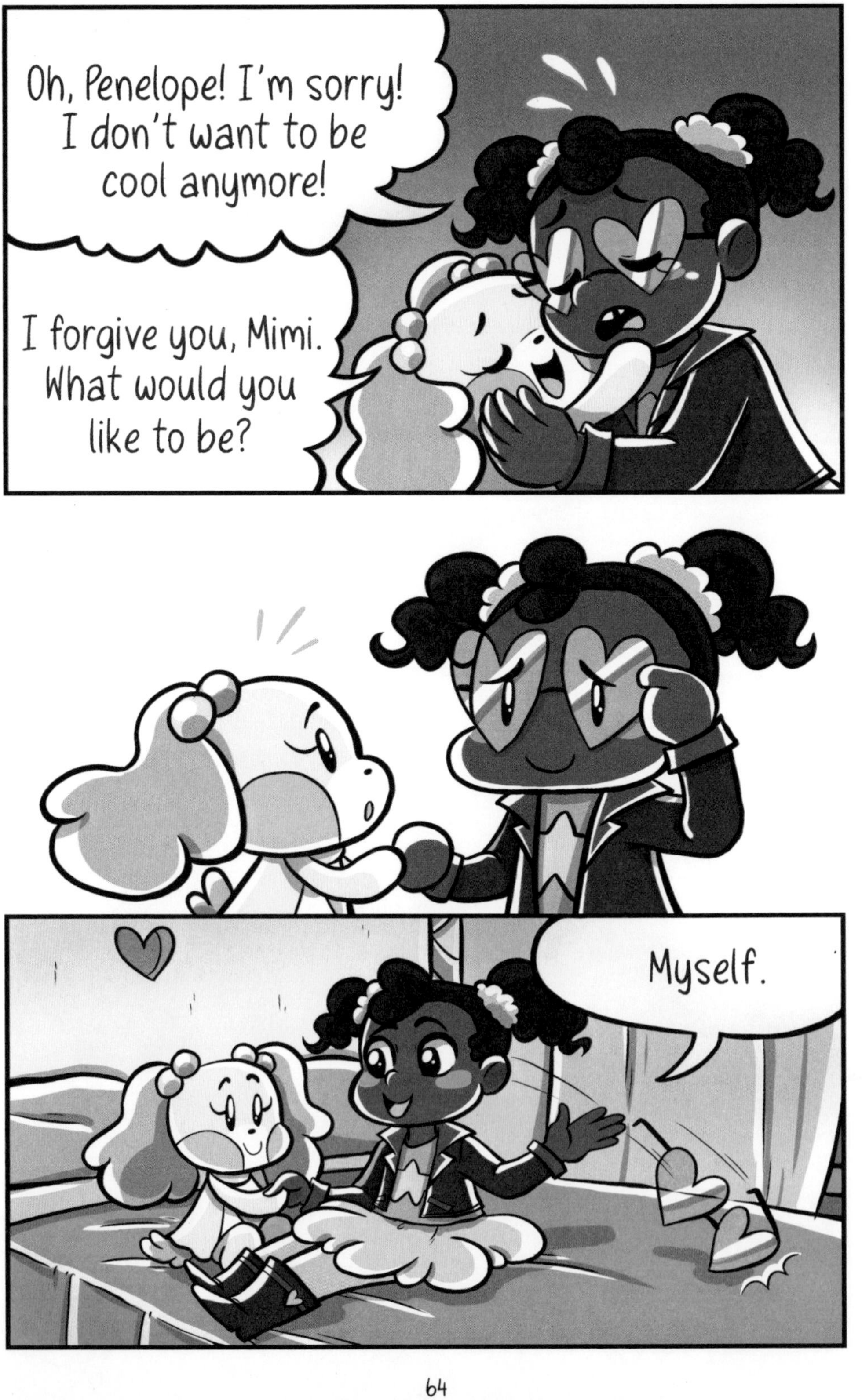
Oh, Penelope! I'm sorry! I don't want to be cool anymore!
I forgive you, Mimi. What would you like to be?
Myself.

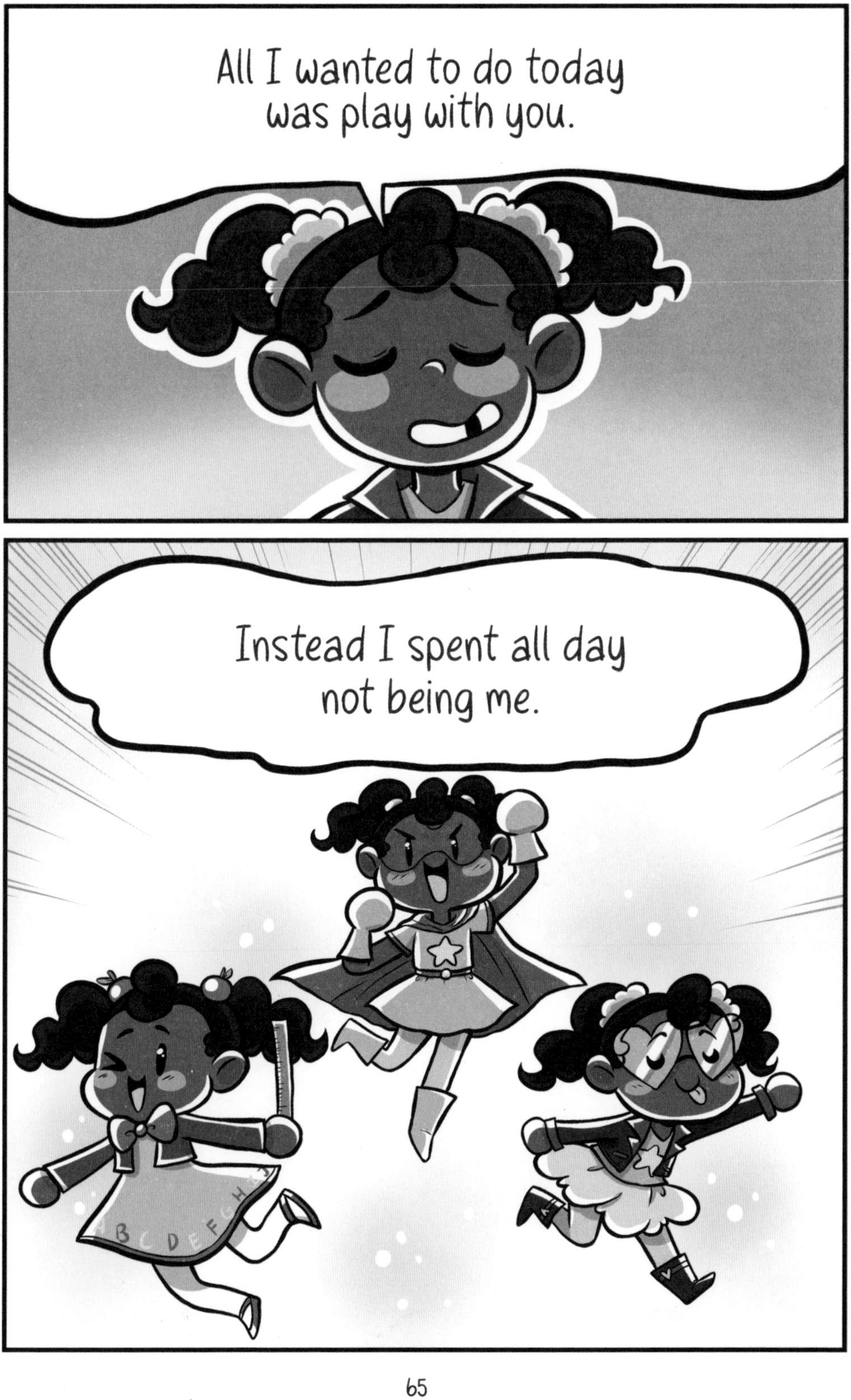
All I wanted to do today was play with you.
Instead I spent all day not being me.

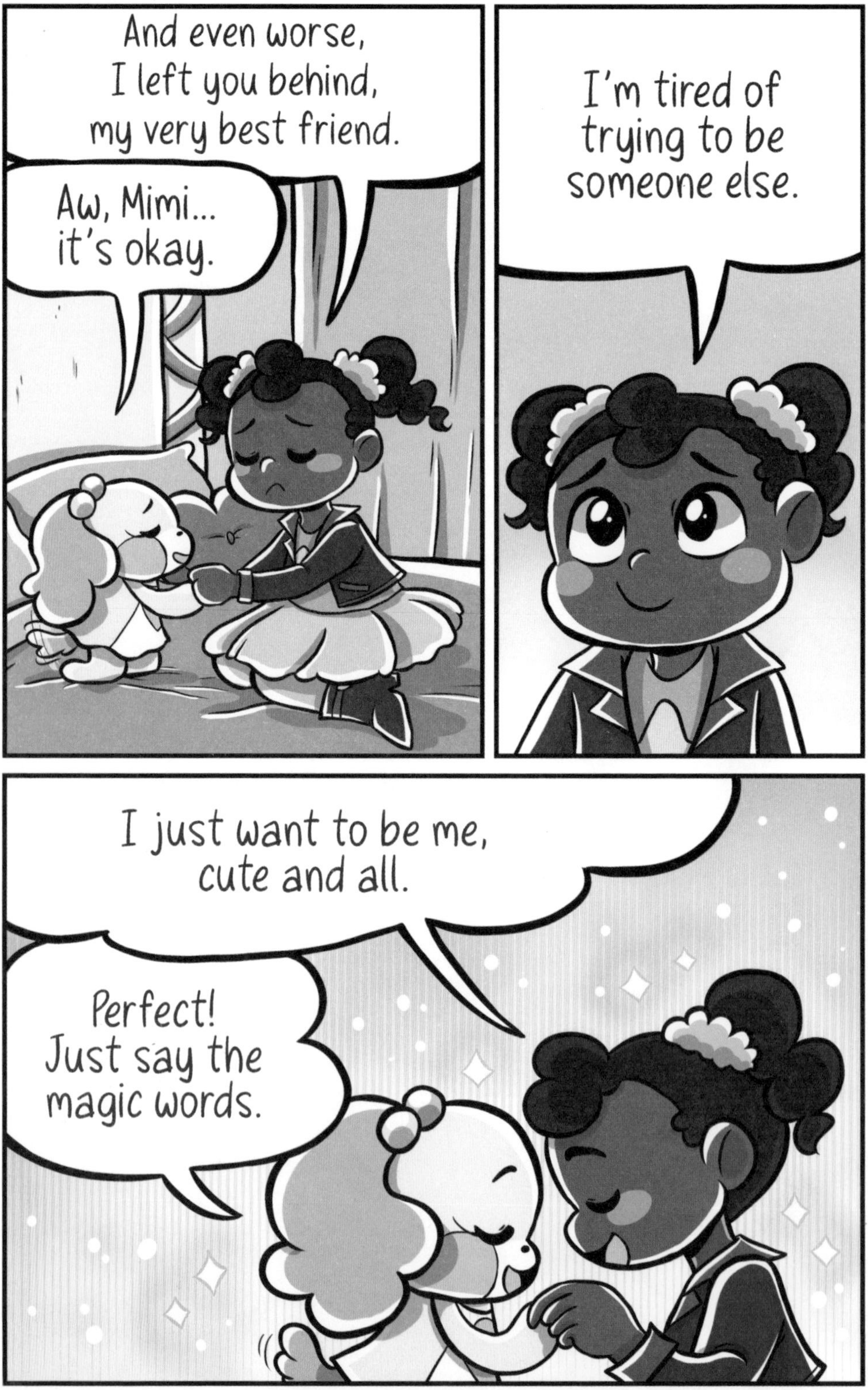
And even worse, I left you behind, my very best friend.
Aw, Mimi... it's okay.
I'm tired of trying to be someone else.
I just want to be me, cute and all.
Perfect! Just say the magic words.

♥ Chapter 5 ♥

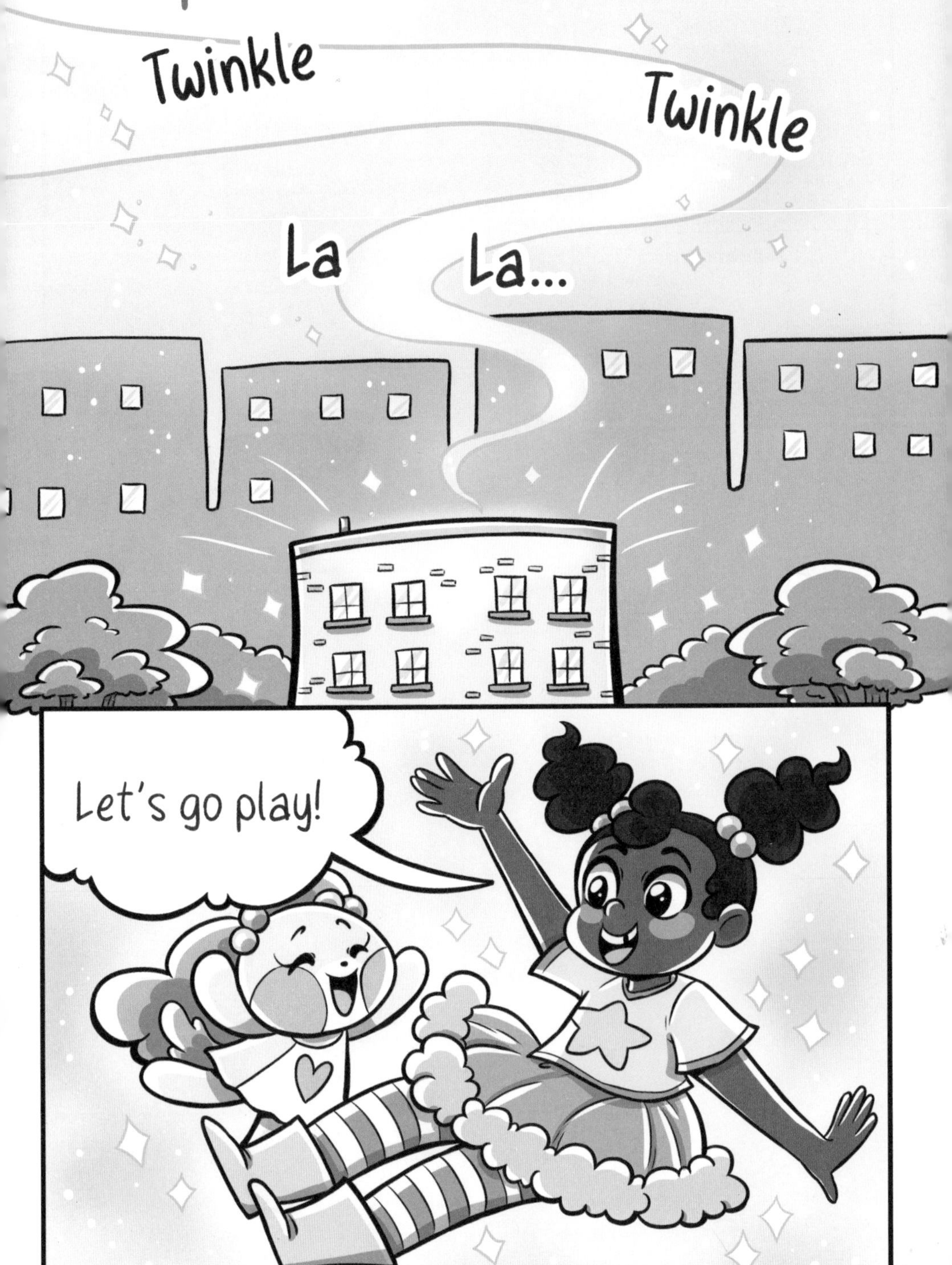
Twinkle
Twinkle
La
La...
Let's go play!

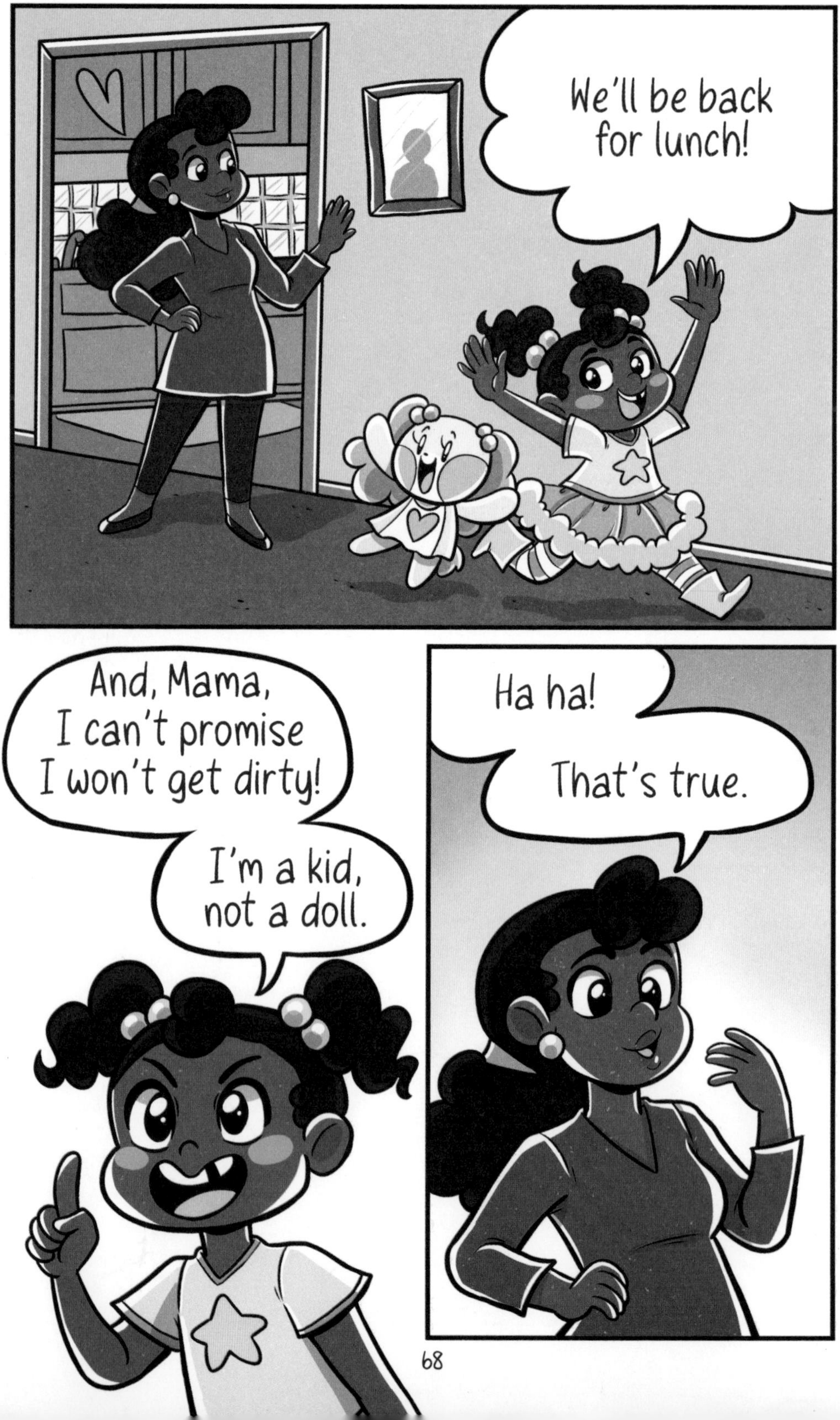
We'll be back for lunch!
And, Mama, I can't promise I won't get dirty!
I'm a kid, not a doll.
Ha ha!
That's true.

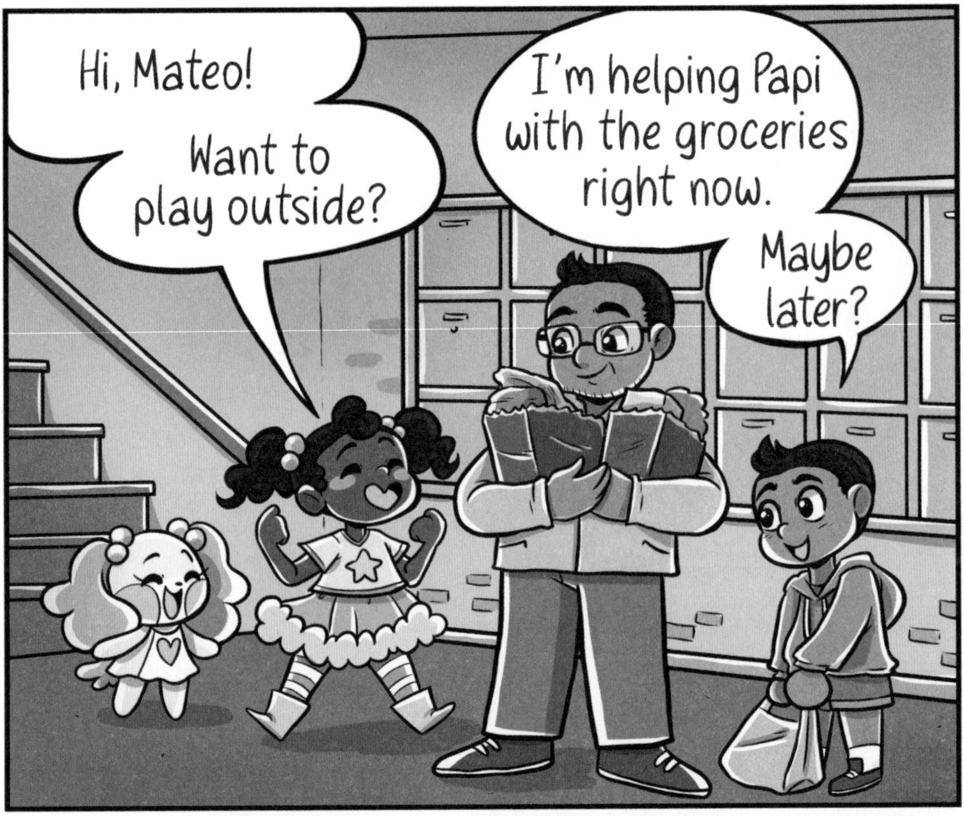
Hi, Mateo!
Want to play outside?
I'm helping Papi with the groceries right now.
Maybe later?

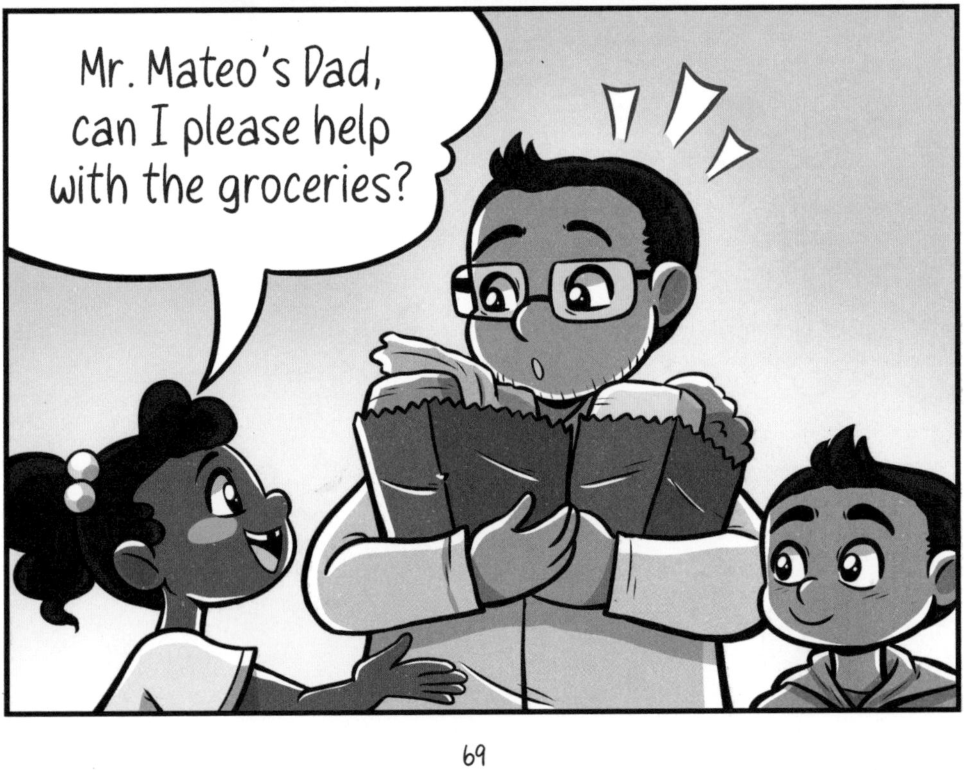
Mr. Mateo's Dad, can I please help with the groceries?

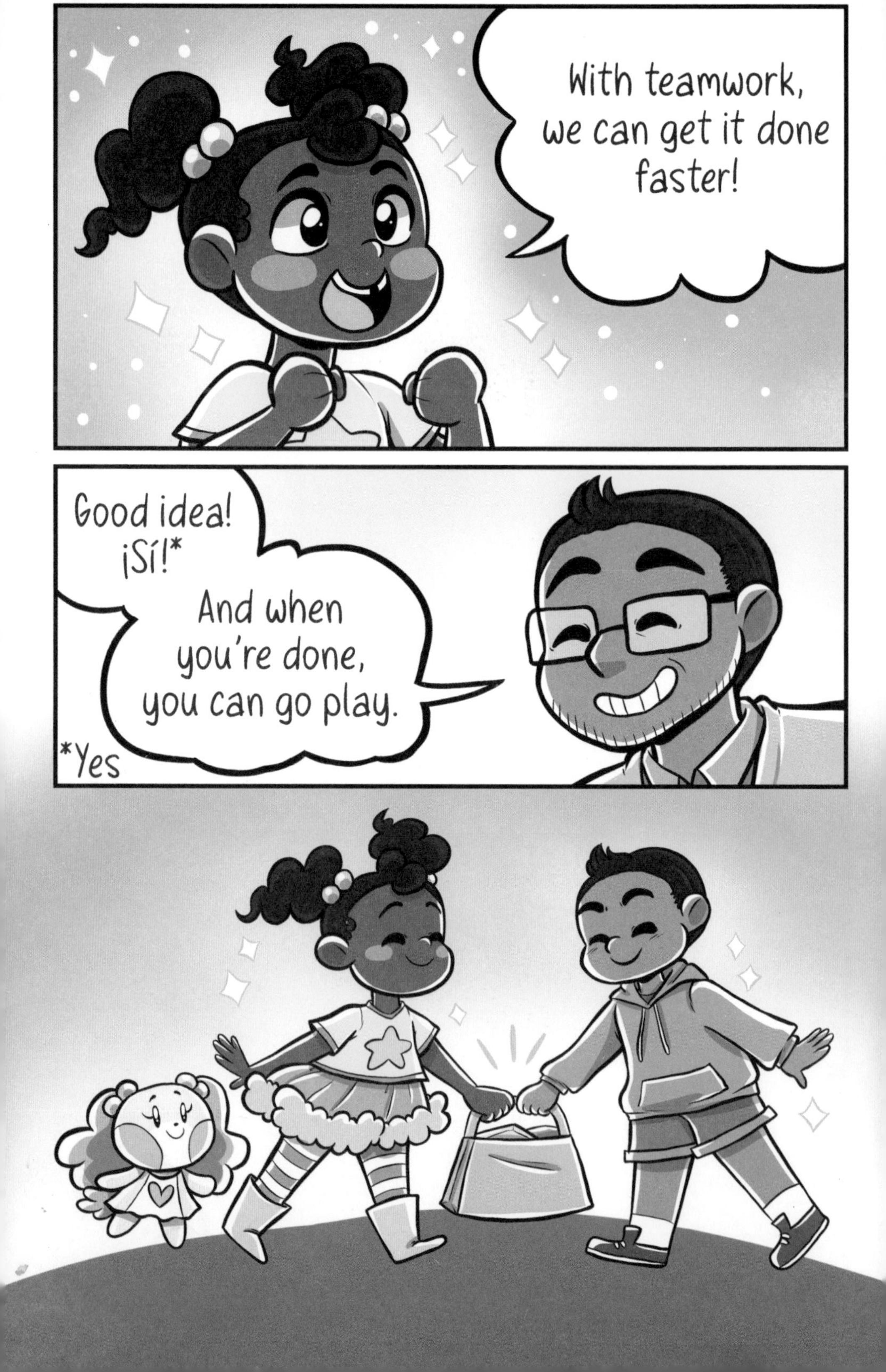
With teamwork, we can get it done faster!
Good idea! ¡Sí!*
And when you're done, you can go play.
*Yes

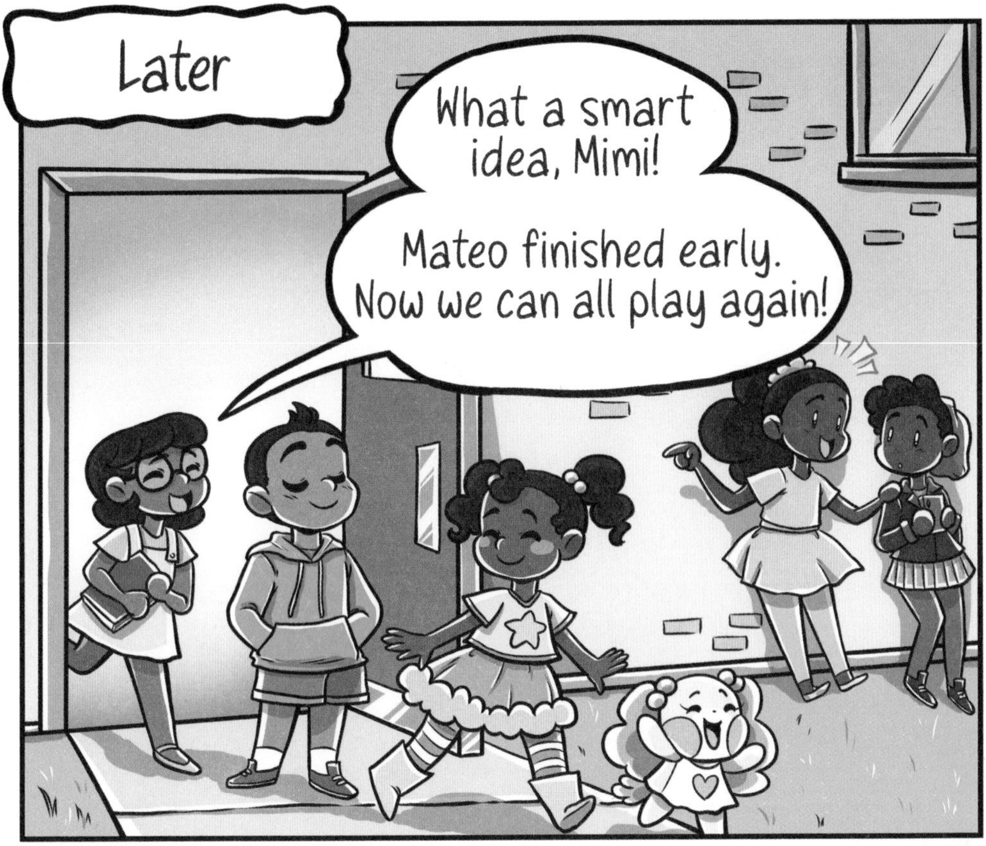
Later
What a smart idea, Mimi!
Mateo finished early. Now we can all play again!

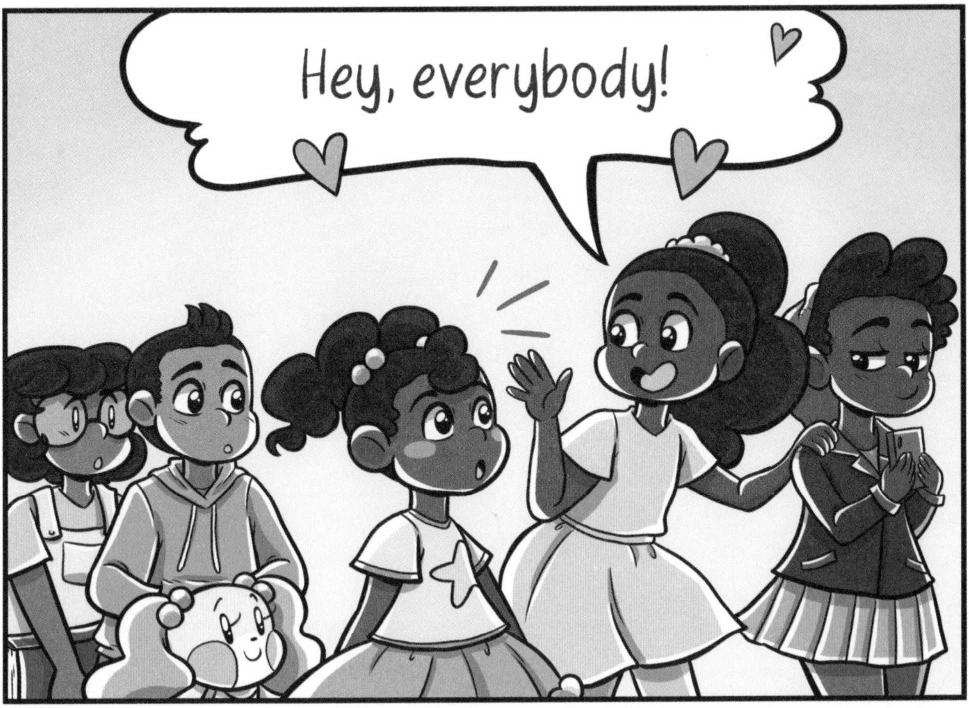
Hey, everybody!

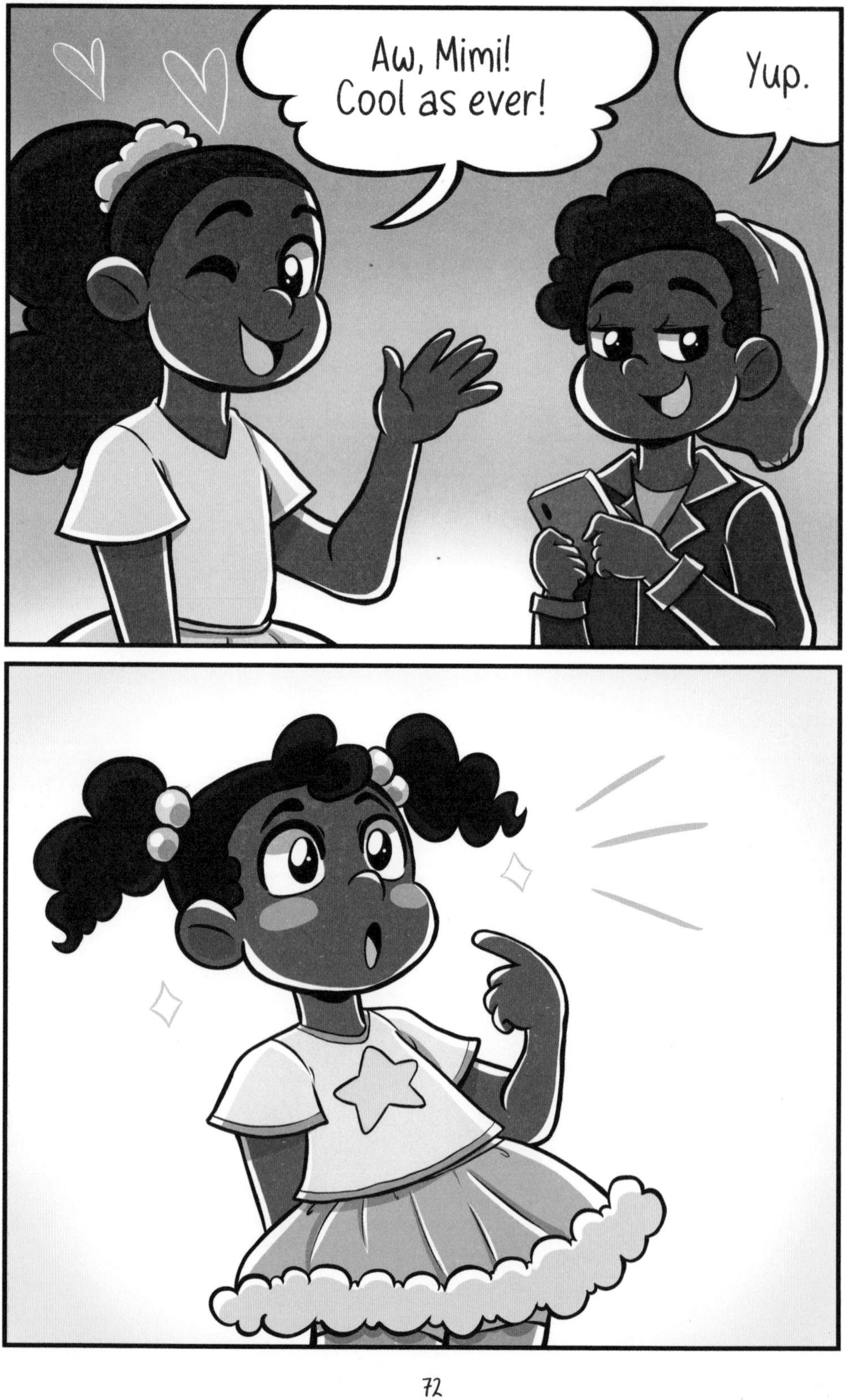
Aw, Mimi!
Cool as ever!
Yup.

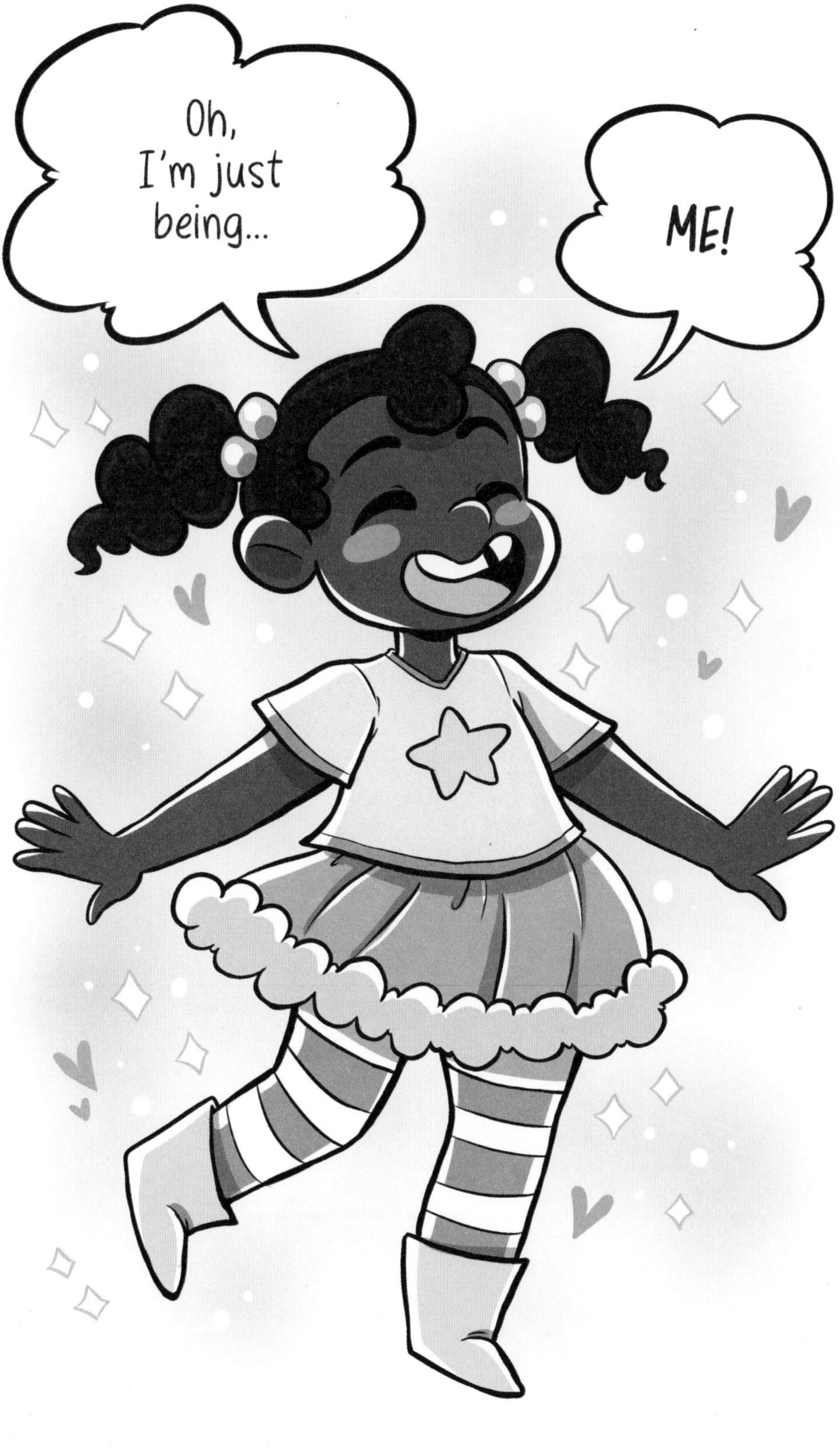
Oh, I'm just being...
ME!

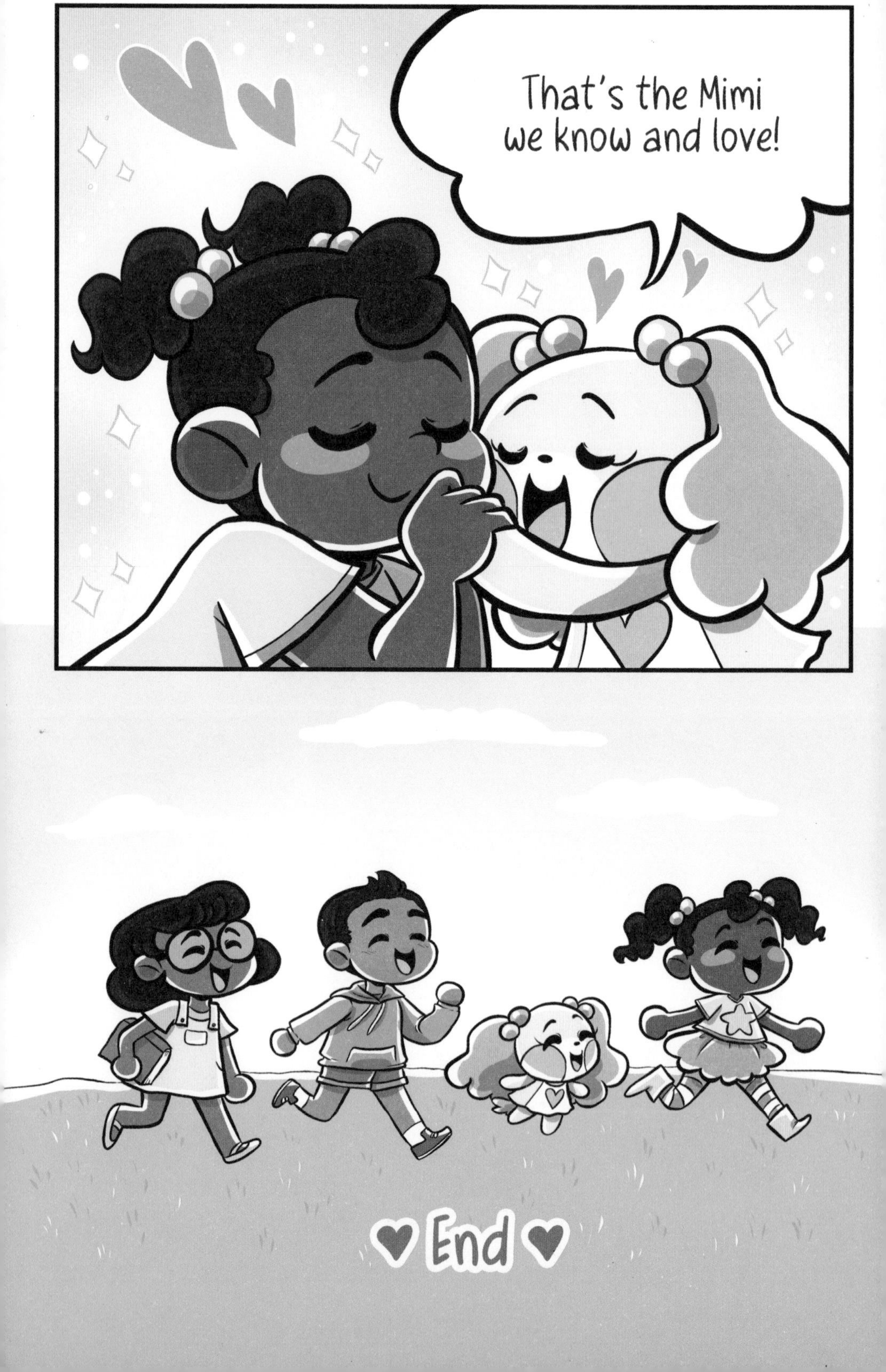
That's the Mimi we know and love!
End

ABOUT THE AUTHOR

With a love for all things pink and magical, Shauna J. Grant is a cartoonist who creates cuteness! Shauna is on a mission to add diversity to the comics community by creating stories that feature Black girls as the heroines of their own adventures, and her work has appeared in *Black Comix Returns*, *Noisemakers*, and *The Secret Loves of Geeks*. She enjoys spending her downtime daydreaming, reading Korean comics, and playing with her own magical dog, Sugarpaws. Shauna casts cuteness into the world via her comics from her home in New York City, the place she was born and raised.